W9-BDP-887

The place was lively as a hot carcass, for the nabobs from the fur companies had come up from St. Louis . . . steamboats on the levee . . . bullwhackers, muleskinners, prospectors, traders, tinhorn gamblers, crews from the boats, new crop of girls all bein' merry.

And to boot, there was a big bunch of Injuns.

The Injuns came in a herd, in blankets and buckskins and bare skins, and so did the whites, all of 'em, includin' some ladies not so damn ladylike they couldn't enjoy theirselves.

You never seen such a crowd.

from THE BIG IT

A. B. GUTHRIE, Jr.

THE BIG IT

and Other Stories

BALLANTINE BOOKS • NEW YORK

Copyright © 1960 by A. B. Guthrie, Jr.

All rights reserved. Published in the United States by Ballantine Books, a division of Random House, Inc., New York, and simultaneously in Canada by Random House of Canada, Limited, Toronto, Canada.

Library of Congress Catalog Card Number: 60-5674

ISBN 0-345-29195-6

Among the stories in this volume, "The Wreck" and "The Fourth at Getup" are here published for the first time. "The Big It" appeared, in somewhat different form, as part of Mr. Guthrie's novel *These Thousand Hills*. Copyright © 1956 by A. B. Guthrie, Jr. "The Therefore Hog" was included in the 1959 edition of the Western Writers of America anthology *Frontiers West*. Copyright © 1959 by Western Writers of America, Inc. The remaining stories have previously appeared in various magazines, as follows:
Collier's: "The Moon Dance Skunk" (under the title "The Fraudulent Skunk"). Copyright 1951 by The Crowell-Collier Publishing Company.
Esquire: "The Keeper of the Key," "Last Snake," "Bargain" (as "Bargain at Moondance"), and "Independence Day." Copyright © 1948, 1949, 1952, 1959 by Esquire, Inc.
Gunsmoke: "First Principal" (under the title "Newcomer"). Copyright 1953 by A. B. Guthrie, Jr.
Liberty: "Old Mother Hubbard." Copyright 1946 by Liberty Magazine.
The Saturday Evening Post: "Mountain Medicine." Copyright 1947 by The Curtis Publishing Company.
Southwest Review: "Ebbie." Copyright 1951 by A. B. Guthrie, Jr.

This edition published by arrangement with
Houghton Mifflin Company

Manufactured in the United States of America

First Ballantine Books Edition: August 1972
Second Printing: October 1980

FOREWORD

EACH of the stories herein, however heightened, has some basis in fact. One of them, indeed, though shaped to the demands of fiction, hews so close to accounts of the actuality that some readers accused me of plagiarism when it first appeared—and one editor was foolish enough to entertain their outrage. So, lest others indict me, I declare that "Mountain Medicine" is the story, with variations on history, of the best-known adventure of John Colter, one of the notables of the Lewis and Clark expedition. John Bradbury recorded it first, early in the nineteenth century. Washington Irving picked it up. They simply reported what were reported as facts. I made fiction of Bradbury's account, staying as close to the record as the short-story form seemed to permit. If any accuse me now, I won't answer. History is there for the writer of fiction, else we have to burn a lot of books.

Other stories were suggested by remembered fragments of my boyhood, by bits of conversation with old-timers and by their reminiscences over a glass or two or three, or half a dozen, and by things read and believed because they were so close to what I'd known and heard.

I had a tall time writing the tall stories. I enjoyed writing the slick ones. I suffered over some of the others and found small, if any, market for them. But if literature is to have dignity, it must enlighten life, and not by sun alone. I am getting around here to thanking whatever publishers there were for permission to reprint.

And, though it is too late now, I want to thank my old, old friend, my father-in-law, from whose wit and western lore I have drawn often. So I dedicate this collection of tales . . .

. . . to the memory of

TOM LARSON

CONTENTS

THE
THEREFORE
HOG

Just once did I get the best of a bed hog, and that was in Ogalally, Nebraska, in 1881 or thereabouts.

He was a ranch cook name of House—Slaughter House we called him of course. The main thing about him, outside of being cantankery like all cooks, was that his eyes was so weak he couldn't tell bacon from beans without his specs on. The specs was as thick as one of his flapjacks, which a man had to sit straight to look over. His mind wasn't that deep, but he thought it was, specially after he had read a book or sucked a bottle. Both of them items was failings of his. He always said he would roam the whole range of writing except his eyes hobbled him. On a bender he was what you might call a hard keeper.

After beef roundup one season me and him decided we ought to put some money in circulation, so we asked for our time and lit out.

Winter came early that year, early and hard, and by and by, with a blizzard blowing that made a man hanker for hell, we found we was there in Ogalally, having drunk our way yonder over trails that was blank now in our minds, specially his. Both of us, specially him again, was saddle-sore from riding saloon and, to heal up on, needed nothing so much as a pillow. Trouble was, people had bunched up in the storm, and there wasn't but one hotel room empty and it with what you'd have to tally as a runt or honeymoon bed.

Now as a bedmate a colicky bronc couldn't hold a candle to Slaughter, which I knew from before. He would jump and wrastle and thrash and heave himself from rail to rail, putting into the act for good measure a fearsome lot of whistles and groans and death strangles. About the time you would think, thank God, he had give up the ghost, he would catch a tail hold on his dying breath and go to bucking and snorting again.

"Slaughter," I said, looking at the honeymoon bed, "who gets the bunk?"

Slaughter's eyes was red and blue lakes that looked like they might flood over the bank of his glasses. Booze made him speak slow but impressive. He answered, "Both of us, naturally. How much range you want?"

"Anyone ranges with you gets the tallow run off of him," I told him.

"You're becomin' damn particular," he said and drawed on his book learning. "Look! I'm willing to sleep with you, not as it's a treat. You're not willing to sleep with me. Therefore I get the bed."

"Therefore!" I came back at him. "Where you get therefore?"

"You got an ignorant mind," he said, standing not too steady. "Therefore therefore. What follers follers. That's how come therefore."

I let the therefores have it, being too frail to fuss much, but it galled me, I tell you.

We went downstairs, where Slaughter said he'd have a little hair of the dog and wound up with most of the pelt. He was a hard keeper all right. Then we ate a bait and

picked up my bedroll at the livery stable and came back
to the room. I spread the roll out on the floor. Slaughter
took off his coat and boots and pants and hat and climbed
into his nice soft bed, letting out a sigh as it gave to his
bones.

There was a little old stove in the room, which we had
stoked up before we went out. Like all stoves in them
days, saving the old kitchen range, it was mighty un-
reasonable, being either ice-cold or red-hot and no in-be-
tween. Right now it was showing the devil how fires
ought to burn.

You know how it is when an outdoor man goes to town.
He can't bear the heat like city people. Too used to bed-
ding down outside with his back for a tick and his belly
for a blanket. Sweats in his clothes and fights off the
soogans. So, cold as the weather was, I raised the window
some. I hung my cartridge belt on a chair that happened
to stand right at the window. In them days I cased my
gun in an open-toed holster, thinking it made me look
dangerouser.

Seeing me hang up my rigging reminded Slaughter he
hadn't took off his glasses. He put them on a little table
close to his hand, telling me he usually had to get up at
night and wouldn't know where to begin unless he had
them on.

What with his blood running anyhow fifty-proof, he
went to sleep right away and right away started his ex-
ercises. From where I was I could see the sky had cleared.
There was just the cold now and the wind, blowing a
little spray of snow through the open window. By and
by, in an hour or so, up sailed the moon, bright as a
dollar. It showed my gun with the frost silvered on the
muzzle of it. It showed Slaughter's big foot, too, which

he had poked from the soogans. It was then my bright idea begun to glimmer.

I hunched out of my bedroll and took Slaughter's specs off the table and laid them by the baseboard. Then I slipped my six-shooter out of its case and drew that frosty muzzle along the palm of his foot.

Slaughter reared up in bed, and maybe you've heard a bear bawl. He grabbed for his foot, which he found, and then for his specs, which he didn't.

"Mike!" he yelled at me. "Mike!"

I let him yell some more before I said, "Whassa matter?" like I was just coming out of sleep. While he was making all that ruckus, I had crawled back to my bed.

"Somep'n burned me," he said. "On the foot. Where's my specs?"

I asked, "Somep'n burned you?"

"Like a brand," he said.

"Slaughter," I told him like I was a doctor, "you ain't at yourself"—which I don't need to add he wasn't.

"Where's them specs?" he wanted to know while he pawed the table to find them. He left off the pawing to feel again of his foot. His voice came out kind of hushed as his fingers found the wet streak that was melted frost. "It left a track."

"Slaughter, old boy," I said, still acting the doctor, "I was afraid of this."

He asked, "What?"

"Whisky," I said. "It's done caught up with you."

He called me a fool and some other things, ending up with, "Think I dunno when I'm hurt?"

"People see snakes," I told him. "Purple and pink and all colors. No use to tell them there's no snakes around."

"Imagination don't leave no track," he said. "Get me them specs! Light the lamp!"

I made out to feel for the specs, though what I was doing was putting my six-gun back there by the window so's I'd be in business again. "They're not here," I announced.

"I put 'em there," he answered. "I know I put 'em there."

"That nose paint," I said. "You got to get off it, Slaughter, old pardner. Promise me you won't take none for a spell. Your foot still hurting?"

He said, "Not so much," like he didn't want to admit it, "but don't think it didn't."

"Sure. Sure," I answered in a good bedside way. "Now go back to sleep. Just go to sleep. We'll find your specs in the morning."

He grumbled around some more but pretty soon went to thrashing and strangling again, getting what he called a good night's rest.

It took him longer on the second go-round to bust out of the covers, but when he did he done it better. It wasn't just the foot alone that came out but a fair section of the tail. Part of it was where the saddle had wore a hole in his drawers. There he was, him and his bare anatomy, and there was my six-gun, replated with frost.

What went on before wasn't nothing to now. This time, from a lying start, he sailed out of bed like a trout and flapped on the floor, yelling like the head chief of the Sioux.

I listened a while and then said, acting half asleep and half sore, "Now what's the matter?"

"It come again," he answered. From his voice you would have thought I was deef.

"On the foot?" I asked.

"It moved up," he said. Him talking so delicate showed how upset he was. "But it's the same thing. It left a track."

"Slaughter," I said, "you poor feller."

He went to begging. "Find my glasses, Mike. Please find my glasses."

"Why, they're right here," I told him, picking them up and at the same time putting my gun back. "Don't you even recollect laying them here? On this teensy table?"

"There!" he said, real indignant. "You couldn't find 'em your own self a while back!"

"I didn't look for them," I answered, walking over and putting them in his hand, for he had got to his feet. "You never asked me."

He hooked the specs over his ears and looked at me there in the moonlight. He shook his head so solemn that he had to catch a step to keep balanced. "Someone's sure got the shakes," he said.

"You'll be all right," I told him. "Get back to bed. Lie down. Probably you'll feel better by morning, though it usually takes three or four days. I'll bring you plenty of soup."

He sized me up again, his eyes swimming with moonlight and whisky and questions, and then without a word he put on his hat and began pulling on his pants.

I said, "Where do you think you're going?"

"Any place," he said, not speaking to me so much as to himself. "Any place at all just to get shed of things."

I asked him what things.

He finished dressing and went to the door. Dignified is the word for the way he walked, the more so because he tried so stiff to keep from weaving. With his hand on the knob he turned round and spoke very preacher-like. "To get shed of fools," he said, "damn fools and them fire snails." Then he went out, closing the door firm behind him.

And therefore I climbed into that nice empty bed.

THE BIG IT

~~~~~~

Two Plumes was that Injun chief's name. It just hit my mind. Two Plumes, a Piegan, and the place was Fort Benton, Montana Territory, and the time somewheres between 1870 and 1875. I had showed up in the town from over in the Deer Lodge country, lookin' for fun but not for what come.

The place was lively as a hot carcass, for the nabobs from the fur companies had come up from St. Louis, like they did every year, to see how much they'd been cheated out of their legal and honorable earnin's. Steamboats on the levee. Other visitors aplenty in town—bullwhackers, muleskinners, prospectors, traders, tinhorn gamblers, crews from the boats, new crop of girls, all bein' merry.

And to boot, there was a big bunch of Injuns, mostly Piegans, but Bloods, too, and other kinds I didn't savvy. A passel, I tell you. Their tepees was pitched out a ways, God knows why, for mornin', noon and night they hung around town.

People was a little ticklish, seein' them Injuns was so many. Give them savages some little excuse, they said between hiccups and rumpuses, and they might forget their manners, which wasn't high-toned at the best.

Then, from some tradin' post, a pack train showed up.

Tied on one of the mules, with the muzzle pointin' the same way as the mule's, was a little brass cannon, or what they call a mountain howitzer.

It took a little time to see that here was the big IT. The trouble with opportunity is that its name's wrote on its butt. But this time somebody seen it before it went over the hill. Fire that cannon, the smart somebody said. Make boom. Make goddamn big hole in far bluff of river. Show Injuns real medicine. Scare devil out of red devils.

There wasn't no argument on that motion. It had just to be put to get a unanimous vote. So the boys went out to round up the Injuns, tellin' 'em by tongue and by sign to come see the big show. Meantime some others said they'd cut the mule from the string and plant him close to the river. Them with no special duties kept circulatin', makin' sure that all hands was informed.

Everyone was, Injun and white. The Injuns came in a herd, in blankets and buckskins and bare skins, and so did the whites, all of 'em, includin' some ladies not so damn ladylike they couldn't enjoy theirselves. You never seen such a crowd.

Like now, of course, Front Street was half-faced, buildin's on one side, river on t'other. The mule men had led the mule to the shore. On yon side was a cut bank they figured would make a good target. The rest of us pushed around close, makin' a kind of a half circle, the heathens composin' one horn of it and us redeemers the other, though there was some mixin' up, it bein' hard to remember it was them that needed to see and get educated.

Now in the front row of the Injuns I spotted this old chief, Two Plumes, that I had smoked with a time or

two. He had his arms folded and the look on his face
that a redskin can wear which says nothin' will ever surprise him, in particular white men and their doin's. The
other bucks was wearin' it, too. You can't beat an Injun
for lookin' like he wouldn't let on that you stink.

The men with the mule got the cannon loaded, one
standin' on a box so's to get at the muzzle and feed it a
whole hatful of powder and then poke the ball home.

So then all was ready save for the sightin'. Aimin' the
piece meant aimin' the mule first and then seein' to the
refinements. Wasn't no trouble. That sleepy old mule
was agreeable. He led around and whoaed with his tail
dead on the target and went back to sleep. With one
man at his head, another climbed up and squinted over
the barrel and fiddled with doodads and got down,
claimin' the piece was trained finer than frog hair.

The ramrod of this frolic, whoever he was, made a little speech then, tellin' the Injuns to look-see across the
far water where the white man's terrible medicine iron
would blow the dust tall. With that, he turned to his
terrible crew. "Ready?" he said.

They sighted again and nodded for yes, and he told
'em, "Fire away, men!"

One of 'em touched a match to the fuse.

The fuse fizzed and fizzed, and Mister Mule opened
one eye and then both, and he flapped his ears back
and let out a snort while the crew hollered whoa and
hung hard to his head. Huh-uh! The mule hunched a
hump in his back and began buck-jumpin' around in a
wheel, the cannon bobbin' its big eye at one and another
and all of us innocent bystanders while the fuse et down
toward the charge.

For a shake no one could move, but just for a shake.

Me, I found myself lyin' behind a scatter of driftwood, and some feller was tryin' to scratch under me like a mole, prayin', "No! Don't shoot! No!" to the mule.

That feller tunneled me up over my fort. The mule was wheelin' and the fuse fusin' and the cannon pickin' up targets, and them innocent targets, I tell you, was wild on the wing or dead flat on the ground or neck-deep in the river, duckin' like hell-divers when the muzzle swung around. But the Injuns stood still, waitin' for the tall dust to blow.

Then, like a close clap of thunder, the cannon went off!

It didn't hurt anything. What with the mule's jumpin', it had slid back, down on the slope of his hump, so's the ball skimmed his tail and went into the ground.

Men began comin' from cover and trailin' up in the dust and the powder smoke, smilin' pale and damn silly.

I walked over to Two Plumes, who was standin' with his arms folded like before, with nothin' in his face that showed anything.

"How?" I said. "How chief like 'im?"

He answered, "How?" and let the rest of it wait, but in that Injun eye was a gleam. Then he said, "Paleface jackass poop."

INDEPENDENCE DAY

~~~~~~

IT WAS July 4, 1920, and Charlie Bostwick was seventeen years old when Bill the Butch fought the Fairfax Soldier. It was a big day in Moon Dance because everybody wanted so to see Bill beaten.

Bill was a young German who had drifted into town from somewhere and had got a job at Nick's Meat Market, where he swept and scrubbed and made deliveries and helped with the butchering at the slaughterhouse that made a stink in the river woods two miles south of town. Nick didn't let him wait on trade. "He dun't spik English so good, y'knaw, and dun't know meat yet needer," Nick explained. "He t'ink too good of himself already, yah, but he fine vorker, you bet."

Nick would say things like that even when Bill the Butch was around, but they didn't seem to bother Bill at all. When he had a chance, he still talked about prize fighting and told what a fighter he was. He was with a bunch of Charlie's high school classmates when Charlie first saw him, at the side door of the butcher shop. "I love fight," he said, looking at the boys. His eyes were bright and blue as blue glass, his face square and simple. "Fight, dat fun for real man. Hah, I vish I be v'ere good men vas." He made a couple of deter-

12

mined passes at the air. "I show 'em. I hit strong, like a kick." He looked down at his thick, stubby-fingered hands and closed them into fists and brought the fists up where he could see them close. "Boomp!" he said, "boomp!" making little jabs with one of them.

Charlie couldn't hold back the question, "What're you doing around here, if you're so good?"

Bill said, "Hah! I take two of you, t'ree, and boomp, boomp, boomp, like dat." His hands came back to his sides, and his fists opened after the knockouts.

In a way his words were a dare, and the boys looked at him, then at one another, and back to him, and Charlie found himself scuffing his shoes on the sidewalk. And in a way they weren't a dare, either, but, what was worse, a kind of insult, said as if Bill was too good a man to bother with the likes of them. It was as if Bill hadn't been talking to them, as if, instead of seeing them, he saw a prize ring over their heads and himself in it and people yelling for him. In the long afternoon sunlight his eyes gleamed.

Bill made another pass at the air, picked up the broom he had been sweeping the walk with and let himself in the shop, his chest swelled out and his eyes still shining and distant.

Afterward George Jackson said, "Jeez, Charlie!"

Charlie didn't say anything for a while. He walked along, thinking and feeling sore inside. "Someone ought to take a poke at him," he said then, as much to himself as to George.

"You want to?"

"Think I'm scared to?"

"You got better sense, I hope. You could lick him in English or geometry, is all, like you lick me, but he would beat you all to hell with one hand tied behind him."

"Stuck on himself."

"Nothing you can do."

Charlie said, "He'll get his some day."

The day seemed a long time coming. There were men in town who maybe could have whipped Bill, but they didn't try. Charlie didn't know the reason, unless it was that Bill was so sure of himself. Or maybe it was that he never talked to a person as if he figured that person could be a match for him, or even figured that the person could see himself as one. Bill's men were all far-off, mighty fighters like you read about in the newspapers. Burt Upham, who was a little old and always smelled of whisky, growled around about teaching a young pup a lesson, but he never did, though he was big and powerful and had been in lots of fights. And the men just back from the war talked mean but didn't act. "Damn square-head," they called Bill. "He don't know Germany lost the war. Like all them Heinies he thinks he's number one."

While they cussed him, Bill just went on talking and making passes at the air going to and from the delivery truck, and after a while it got to be a kind of sour sport just to egg him on. When he came into Gorham's Pool Hall at night, someone was sure to ask about his condition or to ask him to show his knock-'em-dead punch, and a little crowd would gather around him and smile at one another out of the corners of their mouths while Bill talked or shadow-boxed. Like everybody else Charlie wished someone would take him down a peg.

It was the men back from the war and the new organization called the American Legion that finally set out to do it. Charlie heard about the plan from George. "The fight's gonna be the Fourth," George announced. "They got a ex-soldier from Fairfax and, boy, is he good! He was a champ in the army. That's what they say."

"Who is he? What kind of a champ?"

"I forgit. All I know is he's a cinch, and Mr. Bill the Brag sure as hell will count stars."

Charlie felt an eager gnawing in his chest. He said, "Gee!" and then said it again. "It'll be almost like the war over again."

"Just what I was thinking."

"Le's see what Bill says now!"

Bill wasn't in the shop, but came driving up after a while in the truck.

Charlie said, "Hear you got a real fight on your hands, Bill?"

"Yah."

"Gonna win?"

"Sure I vin."

"Sure?"

"I knock 'im out qvick."

George said, "It's a champ you're fightin', you know."

"I hope he stand oop for little v'ile so people get someding for money. You vait. You see how good dis Vilhelm iss." His feet did a little dance, and his left stabbed at the air and his right came over. He went on into the shop.

The town was crowded on the Fourth. The Legion had arranged for a parade and a patriotic speaking and for fireworks at night, but it was the fight that brought people in. The Legion had built a high, solid-board fence around a vacant lot and had set up a ring in it. Charlie and George went in at two o'clock, a half hour before time for the fight, so as to be sure to get places close to the ring. There were no seats inside; everybody had to stand; but the ring had been raised to make seeing easier, and, as the lot filled up, those in back stood on boxes or clung to the fence while standing on the runners at the bottom of it.

Bill the Butch came to the ring first. He had on a dirty old bathrobe and, underneath it, a pair of faded purple trunks. He walked with his head up. He didn't look scared but calm and sure, as if he was as good as anybody and probably better. Bill grabbed a rope and lifted himself easily into the ring. Burt Upham, his second, had a harder time getting up. When he was in his corner he turned around, away from Bill, and gave the crowd a big wink. People laughed because they knew Upham wanted Bill licked as much as anyone.

Bill took off his robe and began squatting up and down while he held on to the ropes. To Charlie he didn't look exactly muscular but only big and heavy and even a little bit fat. His body was white like a grub's, and like a grub's it struck you as something you wouldn't want to feel.

Charlie heard cheers and saw the Fairfax Soldier elbowing through the crowd toward the other corner. When he was on the platform Charlie saw he was a tall, lean man, roped with long muscles. The skin of his face was dark and tight-drawn, his eyes sharp and wary. Under the small nose, his mouth made a tight line. He began flexing himself, too. The pair of them came to the center of the ring, looked at each other's gloves, heard Referee Sam King say something, shook hands quickly and went to their corners. George breathed, "Oh, boy!" into Charlie's ear.

The bell rang. Bill the Butch ran from his corner, head down, like a tackler. He swung overhand, left first, then the right—two long, fierce blows backed by the weight of his running body. The right smashed square in the Soldier's face. The Soldier's head snapped back. He hunched forward afterwards with his gloves before his face and sidled around. When he straightened, Bill charged again. And again it was the overhand one-two, and again the Soldier's head snapped. A trickle of blood started from his nose. Charlie half expected to see fear in his eyes, but all he saw, when the Soldier faced around, was the sure, sharp wariness of an animal.

Bill ran across the ring, flung left and right, and landed again. The Soldier faltered a little at the knees. He clung to Bill, so that the referee had to part them. The Soldier staggered, backing off.

Charlie heard breathing around him, all breaths going into one great, hungry breathing, with yells locked quiet in the throats except now and then for a strained, high cry.

The bell sounded as Bill set himself for another charge. Charlie heard someone say, "Maybe we'll have to ride the son-of-a-bitch out of town on a rail after all." There was a frown on Burt Upham's face. He made a swipe at Bill's face and chest with a towel. Bill's chest rose and fell, big as a bellows, while he leaned back on his stool. There wasn't even a flush on his white grub's body. In the other corner Terry Frimmer was sloshing wet towels on the Soldier's face and chest and standing back afterwards and fanning him. The Soldier didn't take his eyes off Bill. He studied him steadily, as if looking for the weak spot. The water and towels had stopped the trickle of blood.

Bill was on his feet before the bell rang. When it did, he went into his hard, lumbering run and threw his pair of punches. A roar went up on all sides of Charlie, the great, hungry roar that had been locked in the throats, for as Bill struck with his left and right the Fairfax Soldier slipped to one side and brought an uppercut from his knees. The smash of it was like the sound of a bat against a bag of grain. The blow jerked Bill straight. It bewildered him. For an instant he stood with his guard down and took two hard licks to the body before he got backed up and so in position to charge again. Out of the roar Charlie could hear single cries now. "Kill him, Soldier!" "Kill the squarehead!" Bill didn't land one good blow in the rest of the round, and once more he ran into that smashing uppercut.

When he came back to his corner, his face seemed out of focus, the upper lip swollen big under the nose and the nose looking flattened and the bright blue eyes clouded. There were angry blotches on his belly, standing red against the white.

But at the start of the third round he jumped up and charged. It was as if he didn't know any better. It was as if he didn't know anything but the charge and the one-two, and then the uppercut landing in his face and the blood flowing from him now and smearing his face and splashing down on the bulge of his belly. "Bleeds easy, the damn butcher!" "Put him away, Soldier!" "Yowee!" The charge, the one-two, the uppercut, the Soldier fighting relaxed and easy and his tight mouth loose in a smile and his sharp eyes smiling, too, and the white grub gory, and people hoarse with yelling.

Bill went down at the start of the fourth round. He had charged and struck wildly and met the uppercut and, dazed, had fallen before a straight right. He scrambled up fast, as if embarrassed, as if ashamed of himself, as if caught publicly in something bad as sin. He wobbled into his lunge. It was all he knew, the one part of fighting, the single, sorry trick.

Charlie couldn't make himself yell. He felt a little sick. He tried to shake away a feeling of shame, shame for himself and all the whoopers baying their glad whoops. They weren't men enough for Bill themselves, and so they had gone out meanly and got themselves a man, and now you'd think that each of them was whipping Bill himself.

Bill went down, he wavered to his feet, he stumbled ahead, always ahead, making his fists poke out, falling again and making himself rise from his shame.

The final blow slammed Bill on his back. His body made a jerk or two, as if his very will would force it through unconsciousness, and then lay still. The referee counted to ten. Burt Upham climbed into the ring with a pail of water. He was grinning, like everybody else. Over the ropes he said, "There, by God, is a good German." Some men were still whooping, and some were pounding others on the back. A crowd had the Fairfax Soldier in their arms, carrying him overhead.

Charlie couldn't take his eyes off Bill, lying white-and-red, lying in shame, and all his bull's courage dead with him and all his pride.

"Jeez!" George said into his ear. "It was swell, wasn't it?"

Charlie didn't answer.

George hit him on the back. "Swell, huh?"

Charlie didn't quite meet George's eyes. "Yeah, I guess so."

"You guess so!"

"Let's get out of here."

Walking away, through men still hurrahing and passing Prohibition flasks, now, to celebrate, Charlie kept seeing Bill the Butch, beaten and abased and lying like naked while eyes looked on and mouths jeered.

George asked, "You say something?"

"I was just wondering."

"About what?"

"Things."

"Like what?"

"Nothing."

"You act like you wanted Bill to win!"

"I didn't say that."

"Bill had it coming."

"I said I was just wondering."

"You know he had it coming."

"I know he had it coming, damn it! I didn't say he didn't have it coming."

"O.K. then. Let's shoot one game."

"I got to get home."

"Meet me at the pool hall after supper, and we'll go to the fireworks."

"All right."

Charlie walked home, feeling heavy inside and downcast, as if he'd done something wrong. He sat down under the cottonwood tree in the front yard and by and by got out his knife and picked at the turf with it, letting the fight run in his mind's eye and the shouts sound again in his ears while the sun slid behind the house and day cooled off toward evening. After a while his mother called him in to eat.

By the time supper was over he knew what he wanted to do. He wanted to see Bill. He had to talk to Bill.

Bill lived in Nick's house. It was part of his pay, living there was, and maybe it was as good or better than what he had known before, though the room was in the basement and a person got to it by lifting a door and walking down concrete steps that gritted under the feet with the ashes that had been spilled on the way up.

Charlie walked past the furnace to the corner and knocked at the plank door and heard a voice say something. He turned the slick, black knob and stepped in. Bill stood in the middle of the room, holding a wet towel to one side of his face. It flashed into Charlie's mind that the treatment hadn't done much good, no matter how long Bill had been at it. He could see the lips were thick on the side not covered by the towel, and one eye was puffed and purpling so that the gaze out of it seemed small and pointed. He thought the face looked lonesome. There was an iron bed in the room, where Bill had been lying, and a straight-backed chair and a bare lighted bulb hanging from the ceiling and a chiffonier with a basin of water on it and a cracked mirror over it.

Charlie said the words that came to his mouth. He said, "I'm sorry, Bill," and the saying made him feel better. It was as if he had cleansed himself and somehow cleansed the whoopers, too. "You put up a good fight."

Bill said, "You vait!"

"You fought fine."

"Nodder time, I kill 'im. He vas lucky, iss all."

Bill took the towel from his cheek and stuck out his square, swollen face. "I vas soft. No one to spar mit. No place. I get fixed next time. No-good fighter, dot soldier. Ah-h!"

"He fought all right."

"Ah-h! No-good fighter. Already I t'ink how to do it. I train every day. I be ready. I better man, you bet."

"It's all over."

"You iss only friend for me. Maybe I teach you to fight. You can spar mit me, yah. I let you spar mit Vilhelm." The blue eyes waited for a yes.

Charlie said, "I don't guess so. I guess I wouldn't want to do that." He waited to see what Bill would do, making himself hold the blue eyes with his own, making himself hold the thickened face. He turned then and walked from the room, across the darkening basement and up the gritty steps.

For a minute, as he raised his hand to lift the outside door, he hesitated, wondering who might see him come out. Then he pushed the door open and stepped up and out and straightened himself and let the door fall behind him.

There was no one to see him, but up the street, through shadows blurring out toward dusk, he caught sight of George, headed, he guessed, for the pool hall. He found himself hurrying, feeling good of a sudden, feeling released, wanting to shout and run and catch up and throw his arm across George's shoulders and walk with him to the friendly rightness of the pool hall and the later fireworks.

Then he heard the shout again, the great shout breaking from its strangle, and he saw the glad, hungry eyes and the working mouths and one man down who had it coming, and his step slowed and came to a stop at a corner that George had just crossed. After a while he turned half around and began lagging down the street, away from George and the hall and the rockets that would sprinkle sparks against the dark.

THE WRECK

~~~~~~

CUTTER'S LAWYER spoke politely. "Speak, talk up, Mr. Cutter. The jury can't hear you."

"No. I wasn't drinking."

The lawyer nodded his head and studied the notes that lay on the table under his hand.

"Had you had anything at all to drink? Anything alcoholic?"

"No."

The lawyer nodded again and pursed his mouth and studied the notes some more. He was a little man, and old, with a fine head of silver hair. Inside the courtroom and out of it he carried himself with a kind of thoughtful dignity, so that people said, "If you want a good, sound lawyer, get Jonathan Lake."

"To sum up," Mr. Lake said, "you were driving along, entirely sober, at a moderate rate of speed, when the truck plunged out of the side road without stopping?"

"That's the way it was."

At another table the other lawyer was taking notes. He would look up, over his glasses, and then roll his eyes down and write. Mr. McKeever was a good lawyer, too, or so people said, as good, maybe, as Mr. Lake. He acted as if he believed what the heavy young man at his side whispered to him, nodding to it and sometimes writing on his note paper.

Mr. Lake, now, hadn't seemed to believe all that Cutter had told him before the trial. "The evidence is so strong," he had said, looking out his office window as if he could see the question out there, "I have been wondering a little if it wouldn't be better for you to admit you had had a drink or two, but to deny positively that you were under the influence."

"But I didn't," Cutter had cried.

"Sometimes," Mr. Lake went on, still looking at his question, "a concession, a small concession, by a witness will influence a jury strongly in his favor. I'm just wondering, as I told you."

"I didn't, Mr. Lake."

Mr. Lake had looked at him for a long minute, not believing. "The damage suit will be different from the criminal case. We won on a technicality there. It is not to be expected that the judge will throw out this case."

"I can't help it."

Mr. Lake had sighed and nodded and said, "All right."

Now he raised his silver head toward the judge. "I think that's all."

The other lawyer got to his feet. The twelve jurors hitched in their seats. They had been half drowsing, Cutter knew, but now, with cross-examination coming up, they were expecting something worthwhile.

The courtroom was full, or almost, and here and there Cutter could see the faces of people he had been friendly with. There was F. Y. Smith, the retired engineer, a gray, quiet man who carried the picture of his little granddaughter around with him, and Wallace York, the *Messenger* man who sometimes wanted prints made, and Bill Stubbins, who made glorified hamburgers and joshed across the counter with his customers. There were these and others with whom he had passed the time of day, counting them as friends, and they looked at him as a man might look at a bug under a glass, not caring what happened to him but only wanting to see and hear what happened.

Mr. McKeever's voice carried its own answer. "So you didn't have a drink, not even one!"

"No, sir."

"Speak louder! And take your hand away from your face!"

Cutter took his hand from his face. The scars, he knew from looking in the mirror, were still red and ugly. The people at the hospital had said they would get better.

Mr. McKeever went on. "Since our state prohibits liquor, you would deny having had a drink even if you'd had one, wouldn't you?"

Mr. Lake's "Objection!" drowned out the answer.

Judge Stanley leaned forward on the bench. "That is not a proper question, Mr. McKeever. Objection sustained."

If Cutter let them, the faces of the people whirled in his eyes, or advanced and retreated like things seen from a swing swinging high. The hospital had said he'd get over the dizzy spells, too. Near or far he could see in the faces only the sharp curiosity, only the hungry interest.

In a way it didn't make any difference. He was detached from them, and numb, with the real him drawn deep inside him, away from hurt. It wasn't as if his own ears heard the words or his own voice spoke or his own eyes took in the judge and jury and lawyers and the people listening in.

Mr. McKeever was rubbing his hands, ending up each rub with the thumb of one hand squeezed in the other, like milking upside down. "How do you account for the fact that the state patrolman, the intern at the hospital, and the two nurses all testified you had been drinking?"

"I don't know."

"You haven't even an idea, eh? You just don't know."

Cutter didn't. He had seen them come to the witness stand—Bill Wilcher, the state patrolman, and the young doctor whose picture he had made once for the *Messenger*, and the two girls—and they were all friends or at least acquaintances of his, and they all had said he smelled of whisky. He had cried out once, disputing them, and Judge Stanley rapped with his gavel and lectured Cutter with his eyes, and Cutter had sunk back, and they had gone ahead with their stories.

It was all something that couldn't happen to a man, something monstrous and imagined. The bottom couldn't drop out of things, the world overturn in a day, and things combine and friends conspire to make him out what he wasn't. It couldn't be that no one believed him. Not even Mr. Lake. And not even Alice!

Sometimes, with the dizziness on him and the questions battering at him, he doubted himself. He wondered if a man could do things and not remember at all, and then be told and told some more until, out of what he didn't remember, he saw himself taking shape and doing the things they had reminded him of.

It wasn't so, though. It couldn't be so. While they questioned him, while he answered, he put himself back in the days before. It was as if he lived there and what happened now was only in his head, like the things a nervous man would dream up on the edge of sleep and come to himself with a start and smile and settle back again, knowing they weren't so.

There was his little business, the photographic shop, and him tending to it and bringing it along and making friends in the town and putting by a little balance in the First National Bank. It made a man feel good, anyway a man who was a tenant farmer's son and had worked like a mule in the fields before he got up to being a grease-monkey and began studying photography on the side.

Mr. McKeever's finger was waggling under his nose, and Mr. McKeever's red face was glaring into his. "You hadn't had a drink of any kind—whisky, gin, ale, beer, wine?"

"No, sir."

"Take your hand from your face!"

"No, sir."

By and by he had enough money to lease space on Main Street, and he had moved in and had his name painted in gilt on the glass, and business was better than before and he could save more, even with the extra expense.

"How fast did you say you were driving?"

The car made him feel still more substantial. It was gleaming and trim, and people had joked him about it, saying he sure must have piles and showing even while they joked that they felt good for him. It had saved him walking up and down the long street to pick up negatives and deliver prints, and it had given him more time in the shop. More than that, it had added to his feeling of getting on, of being somebody, of being at home in the world. He would tool up the street, and people would wave at him, even Mr. Manning, the banker, and he would wave back or call out hello. He kept the car spick and span, not only as a matter of good business but for what it was and for what it meant, and he had had his name printed big on both sides, "Cutter Photographer."

The finger waggled again, and the red face quivered with rage. "You say you were not doing more than forty? Actually, that was a new car, and you wanted to try it out, didn't you?"

"No, sir."

"Speak up!"

"I didn't."

"You've testified you were alone?"

A man with a paying business and a car could begin to think about marriage. He wasn't too old for marriage, not yet, though he had been a long time working up to it. There was Miss Winter, passing the shop early every day, clicking along on her high heels, and color in her face and her eyes bright, and she would smile at him like she smiled at others, and one day he had stepped out, feeling foolish and afraid, and asked if she would like to go to the picture show that night. They had driven around in the car afterwards and parked on the river hill and just talked. She said she wished he didn't have his name on the car, it made things so public. Alice was a nice girl and a great one to think what people would say, just as he guessed he was himself.

Mr. McKeever's voice beat at him. "Actually you were doing closer to sixty-five than forty, weren't you?"

Speak up! Let the jury hear! Take your hand away from your face! Let the jury see the scars! Forty, sixty-five, gin, whisky. The finger pointing. The eyes glaring. People whirling. People fading and coming on. Miss Winter. Alice Winter. The cheeks red and the red mouth, and the mouth smiling, but maybe no more for him than for other beaux.

Judge Stanley tapped with his gavel. "Answer the question."

Mr. Lake objected, "Your Honor, he's answered it time and again."

"No," Cutter said, "it was closer to forty."

Right now the speedometer read just thirty, and he was driving out the street, headed for Alice Winter's house out beyond the edge of town, and it was fall and he had knocked off a little early and the leaves were just beginning to turn, showing patches and edges of yellow and red in the green, and over the western hills the sun was about to set, and the air was soft, with the burn of summer gone and the chill of winter not come yet. At the corner of Sycamore and Main he waved to Mr. Manning, the banker, and Mr. Manning let himself smile and wave back, and two miles or so away was Alice's home with Alice in it waiting for him.

Mr. McKeever's voice sounded above the purr of the motor. "Now you say you were driving at a moderate rate of speed, you weren't in a hurry—"

He was going slow, past the boys playing ball at Main and Catalpa, and the boys standing aside and lifting their hands at him and he lifting his back and liking to hear their cries, and outside town on the fence rows the trumpet flowers were folding for winter, but the mountain wahoo was coming red and good to the eye.

"Did you see the truck at all? Couldn't a man see a truck quite a distance away?"

A mile now to her house. A slow mile because he felt happy and wanted to savor things, a mile for thinking and hoping, a mile for getting ready. The dreamed questions came to him and the dreamed answers went out of his mouth, the exhaust of the car sounding regular and faithful behind him and the wheel turning easy to his hand.

"And you couldn't see the truck ahead?"

"No, sir."

"Speak up!"

"Not in time, I couldn't see it."

"You couldn't see it, though it had high sideboards, and a horse, a full-grown race horse, was mounted in the bed?"

Cutter felt the quick pinch of fear in his guts, for he had been this way before and knew what happened, but he held it back and drove slow, enjoying things, the buzzard coasting far in the blue sky, the katydids beginning to tune up, the roadside stand with melons on it and the good smell of them drifting into the car—the fullness of time, the resting fullness of time, and the feeling of goodness in him, of coming completion.

It was fall and the leaves were turning and there was the fragrance of melons in the car, and Mr. McKeever's face drew away from his, and Mr. McKeever said to the judge, "That's all." He and Mr. Lake talked to the judge, and then Mr. McKeever walked over the fall grass, through the soft autumn air, and began to talk to twelve men slumped along the fence rows, his voice drowning out the katydids.

Before, he had driven a little faster, knowing that over the next rise he would see the house standing white against the slope, but now he slowed, wanting to see each remembered thing again while the feeling of goodness was in him.

The katydids picked up when Mr. McKeever left off,

and Mr. Lake got up and walked over the fall grass, through the soft autumn air, and began to speak to the twelve men, and the voices of the katydids faded out.

A woodchuck ambled across the road, and a redbird flirted on a fence post. Cutter saw them and saw the red of the maples and the buzzard coasting far off and the road running even under the wheels of his car—but fear was heavy in him now. His eyes strained ahead, trying to see the side road before he saw it, trying to see the truck and the horse standing high in it that he wouldn't see until too late. He brought the air into his lungs and held himself back, counting a fence post and then another, counting the purple ironweeds in the pastures, making himself see each blade of grass that he had run by so lightly before.

The twelve men lifted themselves from the fence row and went outside, and some of the whirling faces went out with them, and Cutter kept on counting grass while Mr. Lake sat down and said, "We made the best case we could." His words went on and joined with the katydids, saying we-did-we-didn't.

Before Cutter got to the side road, before he had finished remembering the grass, the twelve men came back in and stood like fence posts while the voice of the judge sounded. "Have you reached a verdict?"

The fence posts nodded solemnly under their draping of trumpet vine, and one of them stepped out holding a piece of paper, and a voice spoke and ran into the sudden, high squall of the brakes. "We, the jury, find for the plaintiff in the sum of seven thousand five hundred dollars."

The truck reared above him. It had come lurching out of the side road without stop or warning while he counted grass, and it reared above him, it and the horse standing high and great-eyed, and there was the long, quick moment of knowing what must come, and then the blow and the wheeling darkness.

It was morning and work needed doing and Cutter's head ached, and his hands, trying to tidy up the place, were awkward and unfeeling. He put a camera back in the case and dropped an old newspaper in the box he used for a wastebasket and wiped some dust from the counter and looked out on the street still gray with morning and thought again he ought to wash the windows sometime. Maybe tomorrow he would feel more like developing the film that the drugstore brought him because his price was cheap.

Today and yesterday and last year and the years before ran together in his head, none of them distinct or set out in memory, but all like one stream that he traveled up and down, doing again what he had done before, seeing things already seen, thinking thoughts already thought. Like now. Like this minute. It was no different from all the other minutes. It was one with them, and tomorrow he could think was it today I put the camera back and dropped the paper in the box and dusted the corner, or was it another time that was lost in time? And was it today he felt bad or the day before or a day from the stream of days?

Out the window, through a gap in the buildings, he could see a piece of far hill with the long sun beginning to shine on it, and he looked at it as he often did, thinking one day he would go back to the country, one day he would leave people, one day he would go beyond them to the goodness of solitude, to the goodness of the good soil and the good sky and the good winds. He would cleanse himself that way, and free himself. In the goodness of things he would shut himself off from people.

People said this about a man, or they said that, and they looked at him with a look in their eyes, and the pressure of things said and looked grew so great that he didn't stand up against it, for what was the use of standing? A man did, finally, what was expected, and the sayings quieted and the looks softened, and he went in peace, in a kind of peace.

Cutter was holding a broom, trying to make up his mind to sweep, when the door opened and the stranger entered. The stranger didn't speak at once but closed the door after him and stood looking. He had been a big and hearty man once, you could tell, but now the flesh sagged on him, baring the peaks of his shoulders. His eyes, above the hanging fat of his cheeks, looked hollow.

"Is your name Cutter?"

Cutter nodded.

"Mine's Thompson." The man offered his hand. "Had a time finding you. Didn't you use to be on Main Street?"

Cutter set the broom in a corner and stood behind the counter and waited. He had been on Main Street. Back in the stream of days he had been there, back in the day that might be today or yesterday or last year.

"How's things?"

"All right."

The man fished around for a cigarette and finally got it in his mouth and lighted. He sucked a breath of smoke down. His eyes left Cutter's face and traveled across the shop and through the door to the back, taking in the unmade iron bed and the two-burner stove.

Cutter waited. Let the man take his time. There was a lot of time.

"I been meanin' to call on you for the last three years or so." With a forefinger the man pecked at his chest. "Don't get around much lately. Got a bad heart. Came on me all of a sudden."

Cutter said, "I see."

The man swallowed. "I saw your name on the car that day—that pretty, banged-up car. Never will forget the name, 'Cutter Photographer.' "

Cutter saw it, too, with only a little quickening in his chest. He slid back in the stream and saw it, saw it now without hurt, the bright gilt and the block letters, saw it clear but softened, so that he could wait for what the man had to say. He could look out the window and see the piece of hill and think it would be a good place to be. "It was a good car," he said.

"I heard afterwards that they said you were drunk?"

"That's what they said."

"Would you feel like telling me yes or no, honest to God?"

"It doesn't make any difference."

The man put a hand to his sagging cheek. "I kind of hoped you were."

"Why?"

"It'll come out, but it's hard to say what I got to say. Like I said, I been wanting to talk to you. There you were that day, all spraddled out in the road and your face ground to hell with dirt. I was the first one there."

The man brought his hand down and rested it on the glass of the counter and looked through the glass at the shuffle of prints there. When his eyes came up, they were like a dog's. "You ever had to sit back and think about yourself, knowing your time wasn't long, and all you'd done kind of came home to you, until you couldn't stand yourself and figured God couldn't stand you either?"

When Cutter didn't answer, the man went on, "Another car pulled up right after I did, and I told 'em to go get the ambulance or the police. The truck you ran into, the driver of it was out cold, too, but not bloodied up like you." The eyes fixed themselves on Cutter's mouth. "I see the scars ain't so awful bad."

The man's hand went to the cheek again. It was a fat hand, with a tremor in it. "The horse had a broke leg." The words came then in a little rush. "I figured you would die of blood poisoning, if you weren't dead a'ready, and I had part of a pint of whisky in the car and the rest of it in me, and I doused your face good with it."

So now, he knew. Now he understood. The patrolman, the intern, the nurses, the prosecutor hammering at him, the jury deciding while he counted the grass and saw the truck heave up before him. Now it was understood while he looked at the piece of hill and the sun on it. Now it was known while he anchored in the stream and the old hurt pushed out of memory and hurt him again. "Go on," he said, not wanting to go on because, for reasons he didn't understand, he felt the beginning beat of fear.

The hollow eyes looked up, and the mouth, squeezed between its sacks of cheeks, worked again. "In a minute I saw the white patrol car coming down the hill, so I hid my bottle and got out of there. You know how it was if you were caught drunk with a car? How it still is? And I had a reputation to think about."

Pain coming from old pain, and time still like a stopped reel, and the picture of himself on the road and the man washing him with whisky, this sick, sad man with the crowded mouth and the baggy cheeks cross-hatched with veins. It was over and done, the wreck had happened, but still fear stirred in him, a nameless fear of something about to be seen, like the fear of the truck moving in the screen of the side road.

"Go on," he said.

"I don't live so awful far from here, just over to Lewis City, and I saw by the papers you were in trouble, and I said to myself a thousand times, I bet, I ought to go and tell the court how it was. And then I would get scared over what might happen to me, being half drunk and all, and I would say to myself maybe he was drunk anyhow. How do I know? And so I never came."

"You never came."

The man's voice raised. "You got to remember I thought I was doing you a good turn with the whisky. You got to remember that."

Of a sudden Cutter saw the why of his fear, saw it as he had seen the truck, enormous and inescapable, and he smashed into it while he worked the brakes, and above the wrecking his voice sounded shrill in his ears. "Then it just happened! There was no purpose to it! No purpose at all!"

"To the whisky there was, like I been telling you."

"It's beyond. Beyond you or anybody."

"I'm ready to do right. I don't s'pose anything can be done about the lawsuit, but I could clear your name. I could make an affidavit, or go to the paper."

"You can't do anything."

"I don't blame you for yelling. I can say I'm sorry and hope you won't think too hard of me."

"It wasn't you."

"What I been telling you is, it was me."

"It wasn't anybody."

"I don' know as I understand. You're upset. All I can say is I wish I'd acted different."

"Can't you see?"

"Well—" The man held out his hand abruptly, his eyes puzzled and uneasy. "I hope there's no hard feelings."

"No hard feelings."

The man said thanks and swam to the door and opened it out into no-purpose and disappeared into the stream. A shadow crouched on the piece of hill though the sun shone there as before, and, looking, Cutter knew the shadow lay on the sunny fields and the bright waters and in the clear sky, wherever a man might go.

He turned and felt behind a box on a shelf and brought down a bottle and looked at it and dropped it into his wastebox. It was good whisky, or it had been before he had drunk it up.

OLD MOTHER
HUBBARD

IF IT HADN'T BEEN for the turkeys, maybe Clem Randell would have got off to a better start as foreman of the R-5. Still, it would have been tough for him. The boys didn't want anyone taking Curly's place, let alone this big pie-faced man who wore a sodbuster's outfit and looked at you slow and unwinking as if he was trying to get his mind in gear.

I remember him from that first evening when the crew found out that Curly had got his time and wouldn't be back. I can see the broad face with the two deep lines running from the corners of the nose down below the mouth. I can see the calm, slow look he gave us, the lips that didn't smile but weren't unfriendly, either. I remember thinking of him as a man with a face that nothing ever happened to.

Some of us around the supper table grunted at him, meeting him that first time, and all of us got up pretty soon and went outside, leaving him and Rivers, the man cook, in the house. We went to the woodpile, where we were used to sitting on upended blocks and whittling and chewing the rag when the work was done.

"For Lord's sake!" Swede Jorgenson said. "A clodhopper! A regular sodbuster! For foreman!" He got up and put on an act, walking duck-footed, trying to look like one of those sugar-beet farmers that had just moved in on the bench.

"Bib overalls," said Slim Bethune, "and ditch-digger's shoes and a two-bit straw hat. On the R-5!"

We're a hay-and-cattle ranch, the R-5 is, but pretty well mechanized. But most of the boys keep to a sort of cowboy rigging even now, big hats and levis and maybe some brass on their belts. Nobody ever wears bib overalls.

John Goodin was older than most of us by fifteen or twenty years. He picked at his teeth with a hay stem while he talked. "It ain't the duds, boys. You're sore about Curly."

"What if we are?" asked Swede, looking down at John from his lanky six foot two.

"Curly's a good fellow, but mighty unreliable lately." Goodin's voice was low and slow. "You can't put up with a foreman going off on a bender at hayin' time. What kind of a way is that to run a ranch?"

Swede said, "Curly knows more in a minute than this honyacker will ever learn."

"Maybe so." Goodin was quiet for a minute. "How's Curly going to take this, full of tea like he is?"

"That would be something to see," said Slim. "Curly and this sodbuster meetin' up. There'd be bib overalls from hell to breakfast."

Goodin was still working at the doubt in his mind. "After a while a man feels like he owns a job."

I think it was then I knew Curly would come back to the ranch, would come back soon, just as quick as he learned about Randell from one of the bar flies in town. He was a forward man, even when he was sober.

Looking beyond Goodin, I saw Rivers come out of the house, carrying the black-snake whip he kept hung on the wall, and between me and him I saw the reason for it.

A couple of turkey gobblers that roamed the barnyard had got into a fight again. Behind Rivers, Randell came, flopping in those big overalls.

Maybe you've never seen gobblers fight. They get their long warty necks all twisted around each other, like the strands of a rope, until you can't tell which head belongs to which, and they stand and sway while they peck at each other, taking shorter and shorter jabs as their necks coil around.

Rivers always seemed to get a heap of pleasure out of separating them. Soon's he'd see a fight he'd grab his black-snake whip and come running out and crack it around those ropy necks, until it finally came home to the gobblers that something was hurting them worse than they were hurting themselves. They'd flop about and beat the air with their wings and finally get unraveled and run away, sometimes with the blood dripping.

It was pretty funny, all right, except once in a while the lash of Rivers' whip would hit too high and flick out an eye. As far as that goes, though, sometimes they'd pick each other's eyes out.

Well, what I was saying, Rivers came out, with Randell not far behind him, and brought back the whip and snapped it around the turkeys' necks. He flipped it loose and drew it back and lashed again, and flipped it loose and drew back, and then Randell stepped in.

Another man would have hung back, I guess, being new like Randell was, thinking he better get his feet on the ground before he acted, but Randell moved in, almost like he was pushed, and put his hand on Rivers' arm. We couldn't hear what he said, but we saw Rivers jerk his head around and saw his mouth working, and we got up and lagged over to where they were.

"They peck their own damn eyes out," Rivers was saying.

"That isn't a reason to knock 'em out."

They stood there looking at each other. Rivers had his stubbly chin out, like a terrier.

Swede put in his oar. "Maybe you got a better way, Randell?"

"Why—" he said, "why—" and moved over and began untwisting the turkey necks with his hands. When he got them untwisted he kneed the birds apart and said, "Shoo now," waving with his hands. The gobblers trotted out from him, each in a little half circle that brought them bumping back together again about ten feet from him. He got them apart and said "Shoo" again—and it was the same old story. I guess he separated them six times before he finally got one headed one way and one another.

It was sure funny, seeing that big man sweating over those birds, flopping after them and getting between them and saying "Shoo" and having to do it over and over again. It was a fool business that just by accident had got to be important.

When Randell came back to us, Swede Jorgenson said in a voice as mild as milk, "You know, it ain't so easy, puttin' a stop to a turkey fight?"

Randell looked around, his eyes wide like an owl's. "It's no good makin' things suffer," he said.

Afterwards, I went to the barn to turn the teams out. It was just getting dark, I remember, because at first, looking out from the stalls, I couldn't see who was leaning over the half door. He swung it open for me and the horses trotted through and one by one lay down outside and began to roll.

"Stock's in good shape," Randell said.

"Always was," I answered, "under Curly."

"Yeah?"

And then, because I was just a pup and smart-alecky and loyal to Curly, I said, "You'll be seein' him."

"You think he'll show up, eh?"

"Sure."

In the dusk I could see those winkless eyes fixed on me.

"What if I whip him, kid?"

"You won't."

"But if I do? What would it do to me here?"

For the first time I felt uneasy under his gaze.

"It would set the men against me more than ever."

"What if you lose to him—which you will?"

"I'd have to leave. Don't you see?"

"Heads I win, tails you lose."

"Yeah." He was silent for a long time, standing big and dark and thoughtful as the light died out of the west. When he spoke again it was as if I wasn't there. "I don't know. I don't know. A man has to fight, though, if it comes to that."

His "I don't know" was knocking around in my head when I went to the bunk room, where Swede gave me hell when he learned I had been talking to Randell. "Leave him alone, kid. Hear? We'll handle Old Mother Hubbard." It was the first time I had heard the new name.

Jorgenson and Bethune didn't waste any time setting their trap. I caught snatches of their plan that night, lying there in the dark on my bunk and hearing them mutter to each other.

"You think he'll fall for it, sure enough, Swede?"

"Sure. He can't stand to see a dumb brute beat. He said so himself. Anyhow, we can't hurt anything by trying. Oh, by damn, it'll be funny to see that clodhopper on Bullet."

I heard Slim chuckle and Swede say, "I knew a guy like him once, so all-fired gentle with animals, and he was a mean man with men." And then sleep washed over me and I didn't think about things any more until after breakfast next morning when the bunch of us started to get the horses and gear into the field. There was Slim and Swede inside the corral with Bullet, a half bronc that nobody had been able to stick except Slim, who had won second in the riding contest at the Great Falls Fair the year before.

What made us all stop to look was the way they were handling Bullet. They had snubbed him up short, and Swede was working him over with a club, and every once in a while Slim would kick him in the belly and jerk at the cinch, as if he was trying to knock the wind out of him so he could snug up the saddle, and both of them were cussing and making a racket.

Randell had gone to the truck, but he halted with one foot on the running board and watched. After a while, while I held my breath, the foot came off the running board and moved ahead of the other, and then the other moved ahead of it, toward the corral. We all started that way then.

Bullet was plunging from one side to the other and trying to rear, and with every plunge Swede socked him, yelling, "Stand still, you damn jughead!" And then Slim would kick him again. You could hardly see Bullet's eye for the white in it.

Randell said, "What's the idea?"

Jorgenson stopped with the club held over his head. "Ol' Cap's too stove up to use for wranglin' any more, so we're gentlin' this one."

"You have to beat him to death first?"

Swede let the club come down slow and leaned on it. "Mister," he said, "you never twisted this here bronc."

Slim seemed to have the cinch tight now. He turned around. "You got to knock the meanness out of him, or he'll buck hell out of you."

"I never heard of a bronc like that. You're puttin' meanness into him."

"Well!" said Slim. "Maybe you know better. Maybe you would like to top off this Bullet horse."

They had him then. He looked at us for a minute with that still face of his, and then he took a breath and said, "All right."

Along with the rest of the boys I climbed quick to the top rail of the corral. Slim and Swede mounted up with us to watch as Randell tested the cinch, untied Bullet and snugged the reins up in his left hand. He lifted his foot for the stirrup, looking more like a plow jockey than a rider. It was a narrow stirrup, and his shoe was wide, and Bullet kept dancing away from him just as he was about to get his toe in. He hopped as the horse danced, his left foot raised, his right hand twisting the stirrup for it.

From behind his hand Swede said, "This here is known as the clodhopper's waltz."

"Gobble, gobble," said Slim.

I thought we would fall off the rail laughing, but just then Randell got his toe in the stirrup and heaved himself up. At the same time, Bullet got his head down. There was a bow in his back like an angle iron. He was off the ground before Randell ever found his seat, up high and twisting, coming down with a jar that shook your bones just watching. Then he pitched again and the big flopping figure of Randell went over his right shoulder and thumped on the ground. We could hear the breath go out of him.

He lay there a minute while we perched on the rail, and then he picked himself up and went after the horse again. His face wasn't twisted, or frowning, or smiling, or even set. He didn't say anything. But somehow you could see purpose sticking out from him like a flag. He caught the horse and spoke once to him and turned the stirrup.

Broncs are funny. Sometimes they'll buck and sometimes they won't, and sometimes they'll just give a couple of crow hops and then gentle down like a dog. Maybe Bullet was being that way, just notionable, but I had the feeling that in the face of that purpose he knew he was licked. Anyhow, he stood quiet as an old cow horse and let the man mount. Randell rode him around the corral and later through the east field and came back and unsaddled him and turned him out. Slim Bethune said, "I'll be damned!" and that went for all twenty of us.

It must have been a long day for Randell. We had one trouble after another. A team ran away, breaking the pole on a sulky rake. It just happened, of course, that the driver was safe on the ground, getting himself a drink, when the horses decided to break. Every engine in the field coughed and spit and died at one time or another. With most of them, it was gas-line trouble. Somehow or other, hay had got into the tanks. The stacker broke, under a big load of wet hay that one of the bull rakers had pushed in from a slough. And it was pitiful how little we knew about motors or repairs. We stood around while Randell fixed things up.

He spent the day keeping things in order, going from one piece of machinery to another, not getting impatient or mad, not showing he suspected us, but just doing job after job and doing all of them well. We kept thinking he would flare out at us, giving us something more to hang our dislike on. We kept hoping he would chuck it, finding things too tough. We yelled "Gobble, gobble!" when we were off from him, knowing our voices would carry.

Maybe we would have liked him better if we could have got under his skin. Maybe we would have liked him better if he hadn't been capable. And it's certain we would have liked him better if we hadn't been thinking about Curly. Curly would have been shouting or cussing, or singing, putting new life into you, asking you how you'd like a beer along about four o'clock when the sun got below your hatbrim and peeled your lips. Curly was a character, all right.

I got to the barn first that night, being a teamster, and was unhooking my horses when here came Curly out of the house, walking briskly. "Hi, ol' hoss," he said.

Closer up, I could see that his eyes were red and sunk in his head. Maybe you've studied the face of a man who's been punishing the whisky hard for five or six days, and seen something strange there and walled off from you, so that you didn't know how to figure him and felt kind of uneasy. That was the way it was with Curly.

The other men were coming in now in the pick-up, on sulky rakes, and loaded in the flat-bed stacker truck, and Curly was hollering "Hi!" to them. I heard Swede Jorgenson give a regular war whoop and saw him and Slim jump off the truck and shake Curly's hand, like he'd been away for a long time. They stood there talking.

Randell climbed out of the cab of the truck, moving slow and thoughtful as if his mind was far off. Swede made a little gesture toward him, and Curly stuck his head out and started for him. Randell didn't pay him any heed, maybe he didn't even see him, until Curly was right in front of him, saying something I didn't hear. He looked up then, just in time to get Curly's fist in the mouth. He faltered back, shaken but still not looking as if he understood, and Curly swung again.

This time Randell went down. "Steal my job, will you?" Curly asked, cussing.

Randell got up, and Curly hit him again, and Randell fell again. There was blood running from the corner of his mouth.

He turned over slow and got on his knees and lifted himself up again and stood there, and you would have thought he didn't intend to fight back, but as Curly charged in he struck one heavy, clumsy blow, and Curly went over as if he had been hit by a log. He went over on his back, not quite flat, supporting himself by his elbows while his eyes swam in his head. Randell stood a little piece from him, his hands down, as if he didn't know what to do next.

At first I didn't see. I just heard a gasp, as if everyone had sucked in air at once, and then I saw it, the revolver shining blue-black in Curly's hand, its nose pointed at Randell. It leaped in Curly's hand, and a puff of smoke went out of it, and the bark of it rang in my ears. The bullet knocked a wisp of dust from Randell's shirt, under the shoulder. It shook him, as maybe you've seen a tree shaken by a heavy blow. I thought he would go down.

Curly was sitting up. His mouth was tight and drawn over to the side. The revolver in his hand moved and his eyes narrowed over the sights, and I knew, without being able to stir, that he was going to shoot again.

All of us were paralyzed, I guess, standing there with our mouths open and our eyes wide while a man was being murdered. But Randell was not finished yet. For a big slow man he moved like a streak. He dropped below the line of the barrel and threw himself ahead. His fist swung as he smothered Curly, and Curly went out, lying there motionless, the revolver resting a foot from his loose hand after Randell got up. Jorgenson stepped over and took possession of the pistol.

Swede turned to me. "Take the pick-up, kid. Quick! Get a doctor." His eyes went down to Curly, and it was as if he had something bitter in his mouth. "You'll have to bring the sheriff, too."

"No! You hear? No!" It was Randell speaking, speaking louder than ever I had heard him.

"Go on, kid."

"No. I won't appear against him. I won't testify." He got hold of his voice and spoke slow, as if to make sure we understood. "He's young and drunk." I didn't really know, until I put things together afterwards, why my mind flashed back to Rivers and the gobblers and Randell saying, "It's no good makin' things suffer," but afterwards I did know it all went part and parcel with the man.

Randell turned and started for the house, while we stood rooted to the ground. He had taken a dozen steps, maybe, when his legs began to give down. He straightened himself once and forged on, but they went weak again and he stumbled and fell forward in a big sprawling heap.

We ran to him, Swede, Slim, John, and I. We picked Randell up and carried him into the house and laid him on his bunk. "Hot water! Lots of it!" Swede yelled, and we could hear Rivers banging buckets around and working the pump handle and shaking down the range.

We straightened Randell out and got his bloody shirt loose while he looked at us out of a pale sick face, not saying anything. The hole looked pretty high, but a good deal of blood had run out of it front and back.

"Rags! Clean ones!" Swede said to John Goodin.

The boys had all crowded into the bunk room and stood there silent. By and by one of them took off his hat, and one by one they all did, as if at a funeral or something. It struck me sudden and strange that deep in my gizzard I was hoping for Randell not to die.

Then the screen door banged, and it was Curly, coming in wild-eyed and red in the face. Our eyes went to him, and our silence broke against him; he pulled himself up, and his mouth began to run with words. "I thought he had a gun. He made as if to pull a pistol."

Nobody said a word. Jorgenson looked at Curly long and slow. There was hurt in that big Swede's face and something else, something old and sad and wise.

He didn't speak to Curly, but he turned and put his hand on Randell and said, "Take it easy, old-timer. You're gonna be O.K." I felt a shout leaping into my throat, for all at once I just knew in my bones he had to be O.K., but I didn't let the shout out, because just then Jorgenson's eyes came around and saw me and his voice rose big and stormy in the room. "Damn you, kid! I told you once. Get goin' for the doc!"

EBBIE

EBONY, the Gordon setter, was in heat again, and a bunch of dogs were always hanging around the Bostwick house. From the window Charlie could see the Jacksons' yellow cur, Tip, and the bulldog that the Johnsons had sent east for and the Bowmars' little Sprite and four or five others, some of which he wasn't sure of. Sometimes they fought, but not often. Mostly they were friendly and patient, lying with their tongues hanging out and their eyes on the back door, or one after the other cocking their legs against the old cottonwood tree or the axe-marked chopping block that Father cut the firewood on.

Because old Eb was in heat, Father was out of humor with her. Coming home from the office and seeing all the dogs lying around, he walked stiff and kept his eyes on the ground as if Eb was bringing shame on the house. It was the same in the morning when he set out for work and maybe found Tip lying just outside the door. He would aim a sudden kick at him and go on while words sounded in his throat.

Charlie didn't know what made Father feel that way. Grown-ups had reasons of their own that you wouldn't understand until you were grown up yourself. Until then you didn't ask and you didn't object; you just wondered, like wondering why Father sometimes was full of play and tricks, and it was like the sun shining inside the house, and then at other times, for no cause that a boy could understand, he was touchy and short-tempered, and it was like a thundercloud had come across the sun.

Charlie sat down on the floor and let his hand run over the thick, silky curl of Eb's coat. She was tipped with gold, but most of her was watered black. She looked at him out of her good eye, and her tail made a slow pat on the floor. The other eye had been put out by birdshot long ago, before Charlie could remember. There was just the hole there and the lids half closed and the meat showing a little behind them and always a little wet streak down her muzzle where the eye drained. Father said he had tried to dust her, when they were out hunting, because she ranged too far, and one of the shot had happened to get her in the eye.

Eb loved Father, maybe understanding him better than a boy could. She loved the smell of his hunting jacket and the sound his shotgun made as he tried the pump before setting out for prairie chickens or mallards or geese. She would prance crazily around him and whine almost like talking, and he would smile and say, "All right, old girl. All right."

Father said maybe Eb didn't have the best nose in the world, but he would like to see her equal at retrieving. She would go anywhere to get his birds and bring them and lay them at his feet without a tooth mark on them. Charlie thought she must have a pretty good nose at that or she wouldn't find anything at all, not with just one good eye. He would try her out himself as soon as he was old enough to carry a gun. He felt old enough now, at nine years, but Mamma said he would have to wait until he was twelve at least. So all he could do was play with Eb. He had broken her to lead and to pull a wagon, and she would scratch like everything for him, trying to dig a gopher out. He bet that next to hunting she liked to be with him best, tagging at his heels or retrieving the sticks he threw or just lying with him behind the big range in the kitchen where the slow warmth sometimes put them both to sleep.

Outside, the day was dimming off toward dark. The dogs were all lying down, some of them with their eyes closed but with their ears alive and listening. Father was probably on his way home by now.

Charlie got up and put on his sweater and went to the kitchen to go outside. His mother turned from her work board, the ends of her fingers lumpy with dough, and smiled at him. She said, "Don't go far. It'll be suppertime before long."

"I'm just going out."

"What for?"

"Well, I thought—you see, Father doesn't like the dogs in the yard, and I thought—"

She turned back to the board, and it was a little time before she spoke. Then she said, "I see, dear. Watch Eb doesn't go out with you."

Eb tried to follow him, her heavy brush of tail wagging hopefully, but he kneed her back and closed the door. He had stored a handful of rocks by the step, and now he picked them up, yelled, "Get out of here!" and began pegging the stones at the dogs, throwing easy and not very straight. The dogs slid out of range and stopped and grinned at him.

Father was silent at the supper table, thinking thoughts

and feeling things Charlie couldn't guess. Once he asked, "Where's Eb?" and Mamma answered, "On the back porch. I latched the door," and Father went on eating and thinking. The porch was boarded up for three feet or so and screened the rest of the way to the top.

It had grown darker, so dark you couldn't see out the window from the lighted room, but Charlie knew the dogs had come back. He knew it even before he heard the sounds of the fight. Father's face clouded. "Those dogs!"

It was Mamma who found later that Eb had got out. She opened the door to the porch and turned back and stood with a still and startled look on her face, and the knowledge of what had happened leaped up in Charlie and clutched his insides. He started to whisper, "I'll find her," but Father came into the kitchen just then and caught the still and startled look, too, and asked, "What's wrong?" and looked outside and saw where Eb had made a hole through the screen.

Father went over to the corner where Charlie had leaned his ball bat and picked it up and said, "Come along, son! You can help locate her."

Two up-and-down lines marked Mamma's forehead, between the eyes. "Please, Harold," she said, and added, "It's just natural," but Father acted as if he didn't hear her. He slammed through the screen door with the bat held tight in his hand.

They found Eb right away, at the rear of the vacant lot next to their house. To Charlie it seemed there must have been a hundred dogs around. Some of them were just shapes at the edge of darkness. One was on top of Eb. Father ran up, waving the bat. It was the Jacksons' dog, Tip, that was on top. Father swung at him and missed, and Tip leaped off and jumped away and stood waiting, his eyes sharp and his mouth open and his hanging tongue looking dark in the half-dark.

Father grabbed Eb by the collar and started jerking her back toward the house. When his back was turned, Tip ran up again and rose on his hind legs and began hugging Eb with his front ones. Eb hung back, and Father turned and saw what was happening and swung the bat at Tip and, after he had missed again, raised it high and brought it down on Eb's head. The solid whack of it was drowned out by the howl that burst out of Eb. It was a high, shrill, wavy howl that hurt the ears like a whistle, and it went on and on, not stopping even for a breath.

Father jerked her ahead again and dragged her up the steps and flung her toward the rag rug on the porch. Then he moved the woodbox over so that it covered the hole she had made in the screen. "She won't want to be getting out again this night, I'm thinking," he said in a voice that made Charlie's stomach draw up.

Mamma looked at him when they came in the house, and Father said, still in that hard, ungiving tone, "I made a dead dog out of my dog, almost." Eb's crying reached inside the house. It sounded a little weaker here, but it still hurt the ears and it still went on and on as if the pain in her never let up even for a swallow or a gulp of air.

Mamma's voice was so quiet it made Charlie look at her. "I don't know why you let yourself get into these blind rages. You've made a dog out of yourself, I'm afraid." Charlie saw that her face was white and that the hands over the dishpan trembled. He never had heard her speak to Father that way before, and he drew back inside himself, expecting a fierce answer, but Father didn't say a word. He turned and walked from the room.

"You get ready for bed, son," Mamma said, not looking at him.

Before he went to school the next morning, Charlie found what had made Eb howl. He had gone to tell her good-by, and her tail thumped on the floor for him, and she raised her old head. He held still, unbelieving, and the breath in him held still, too, while the fact beat against him. He saw the blind eye and the glimmer of red behind the lids, but what he couldn't believe he saw was the other eye, blind now, too, and empty-socketed, and the seepage from it making an unclean furrow down her nose.

He didn't cry. There were no tears in him, only a feeling of emptiness, only the feeling of unbelieving. He dropped down and brought her head into his lap and couldn't look at the eye again. "Oh, Ebbie," he whispered, "why did you have to do it? Why did you have to go and do it, Ebbie?" She let her head rest in his lap, and her tail wagged on as always, but slower, Charlie thought, than he had ever seen it.

Mamma called from inside, "You'll be late for school, Charlie," and he got up, not answering, and picked up his books and made his feet take him away. He couldn't tell anyone what had happened, not even Mamma. He had to hold it tight inside himself, a cold secret that lay in his stomach like a weight all day.

Coming back after school, he saw the dogs in the back yard again, and a sudden fury came on him. He gathered up a big handful of rocks and sneaked up and began throwing hard and straight as he could, feeling a fierce biting inside his chest when one of the stones brought a yelp from Tip.

Inside, he still couldn't tell Mamma about Eb, though he wondered if the knowing of it wasn't what made her quiet and gentler, even, than usual. He refused the cookies she offered and afterward stole out to the porch. It was true. The secret was still true. He got Eb's head in his lap again.

Father was late getting home. The sun had gone beyond the mountains and the light was fading out of things before Charlie heard his step. Charlie slipped into the bathroom, leaving the door open just a crack, not wanting to see Father now, not wanting Father to see his face and read the secret in it. The front door opened and closed, and Charlie heard the rustle of clothing as Father took off his topcoat. He heard Mama coming from the kitchen and then her voice, sounding low but not sharp, sounding low and gentle. "Ebbie's blind, Harold. Her other eye's out. I don't know what to tell Charlie. Maybe he knows already." The voice faltered before it got through.

There was a long silence. In his mind Charlie could see Father, standing with his head bent and his mouth set while he thought. The silence grew into a ringing in the ears, and then Father's step broke it, lagging toward the kitchen.

Mamma's voice was just above a whisper. "What are you going to do?"

"There's only one thing." Father's steps went on.

Charlie flung open the bathroom door and ran out. Mamma wasn't to the kitchen yet. She turned and said, "Charlie."

He cried out, "I know. I know. I've got to see!"

"I wish you wouldn't go."

"I've got to."

Her hand, uplifted in a little movement, stayed him for an instant. Her eyes searched his face. "Don't be angry, Charlie. Don't feel hard toward Father. Try to understand. He's sorry, sorrier than you can know."

"Why'd he do it then?"

"He couldn't help himself. Don't you see, he couldn't help himself?" He saw tears shining in her eyes and her mouth trembling.

"I got to go," he cried out again, and dodged her and ran to the kitchen.

Father was on the back porch. He had his shotgun in one hand and Eb's head held up in the other, looking to make sure, Charlie guessed, that the good eye wasn't good any more. He let the head down and took hold of the collar and said, "Come on, girl," and, turning, saw Charlie. "You stay back, son!"

"I got to see, I tell you. I got to see."

Father didn't say any more. He just breathed deep and started leading Eb off the porch. She bumped against the door frame as they went out. The dogs lying in the back yard got up and backed off, watching.

Father took Eb over to the vacant lot, almost to where they had found her yesterday. The dogs trailed after them, Tip in the lead.

Father's hand worked the pump, throwing a shell in the chamber, and Eb's tail waved at the sound of it. Charlie thought if she could see she would be prancing.

"Sit down, girl. Sit down."

She let her hindquarters down and looked up at Father out of her blind eyes, and her tail waved again. In the dusk Charlie could see the ugly furrow that the matter from her hurt eye made.

Father stepped back. The shotgun was a long time coming up. Charlie couldn't look when it was leveled. He couldn't believe he stood there in the dark waiting for the shot, waiting for Eb to be killed, waiting for this cold and awful end.

The roar of the gun shook him. It brought his head around. Eb had sunk to the ground. A little twitching was running over her body. After a minute it stopped, and Eb didn't stir at all except for one curl of hair moving to a breath of air.

Father went over to her and stooped and put his hand out and rested it on her side. He didn't speak, not for a long time, but just stooped and let his hand lie soft and kind on her side. He moved his head a little, and Charlie saw the side of his face downturned to the ground, and of a sudden it seemed to the boy he had never seen the face before, never seen the sadness there and the kindness, too, and the marks of wild, dark angers that he couldn't help.

Father's voice sounded tired. "Run to the woodshed and get the spade, will you, son?"

When Charlie hesitated, Father said, "We'll dig a grave under the Balm of Gilead. I think she'd like to lie there."

Charlie turned and ran for the woodshed, and a great sob formed in his stomach and tore at his throat and burst out of him. He got around the corner of the shed, where Father wouldn't see him, and his legs let him down on the chopping block. He thought that all his life he would see Eb sinking to the ground and Father's sad, dark face downturned on her and the tears in Mamma's eyes. He didn't know for whom he cried, for Eb or Father or Mother or himself. He only knew, while sobs racked him and the tears streamed down his cheeks and put the taste of salt in his mouth, that now he had to cry.

BARGAIN

Mr. Baumer and I had closed the Moon Dance Mercantile Company and were walking to the post office, and he had a bunch of bills in his hand ready to mail. There wasn't anyone or anything much on the street because it was suppertime. A buckboard and a saddle horse were tied at Hirsch's rack, and a rancher in a wagon rattled for home ahead of us, the sound of his going fading out as he prodded his team. Freighter Slade stood alone in front of the Moon Dance Saloon, maybe wondering whether to have one more before going to supper. People said he could hold a lot without showing it except in being ornerier even than usual.

Mr. Baumer didn't see him until he was almost on him, and then he stopped and fingered through the bills until he found the right one. He stepped up to Slade and held it out.

Slade said, "What's this, Dutchie?"

Mr. Baumer had to tilt his head up to talk to him. "You know vat it is."

Slade just said, "Yeah?" You never could tell from his face what went on inside his skull. He had dark skin and shallow cheeks and a thick-growing mustache that fell over the corners of his mouth.

61

"It is a bill," Mr. Baumer said. "I tell you before it is a bill. For twenty-vun dollars and fifty cents."

"You know what I do with bills, don't you, Dutchie?" Slade asked.

Mr. Baumer didn't answer the question. He said, "For merchandise."

Slade took the envelope from Mr. Baumer's hand and squeezed it up in his fist and let it drop on the plank sidewalk. Not saying anything, he reached down and took Mr. Baumer's nose between the knuckles of his fingers and twisted it up into his eyes. That was all. That was all at the time. Slade half turned and slouched to the door of the bar and let himself in. Some men were laughing in there.

Mr. Baumer stooped and picked up the bill and put it on top of the rest and smoothed it out for mailing. When he straightened up I could see tears in his eyes from having his nose screwed around.

He didn't say anything to me, and I didn't say anything to him, being so much younger and feeling embarrassed for him. He went into the post office and slipped the bills in the slot, and we walked on home together. At the last, at the crossing where I had to leave him, he remembered to say, "Better study, Al. Is good to know to read and write and figure." I guess he felt he had to push me a little, my father being dead.

I said, "Sure. See you after school tomorrow" —which he knew I would anyway. I had been working in the store for him during the summer and after classes ever since pneumonia took my dad off.

Three of us worked there regularly, Mr. Baumer, of course, and me and Colly Coleman, who knew enough to drive the delivery wagon but wasn't much help around the store except for carrying orders out to the rigs at the hitchpost and handling heavy things like the whisky barrel at the back of the store which Mr. Baumer sold quarts and gallons out of.

The store carried quite a bit of stuff—sugar and flour and dried fruits and canned goods and such on one side and yard goods and coats and caps and aprons and the like of that on the other, besides kerosene and bran and buckets and linoleum and pitchforks in the storehouse at the rear—but it wasn't a big store like Hirsch Brothers up the street. Never would be, people guessed, going on to say, with a sort of slow respect, that it would have gone under long ago if Mr. Baumer hadn't been half mule and half beaver. He had started the store just two years before and, the way things were, worked himself close to death.

He was at the high desk at the end of the grocery counter when I came in the next afternoon. He had an eyeshade on and black sateen protectors on his forearms, and his pencil was in his hand instead of behind his ear and his glasses were roosted on the nose that Slade had twisted. He didn't hear me open and close the door or hear my feet as I walked back to him, and I saw he wasn't doing anything with the pencil but holding it over paper. I stood and studied him for a minute, seeing a small, stooped man with a little paunch bulging through his unbuttoned vest. He was a man you wouldn't remember from meeting once. There was nothing in his looks to set itself in your mind unless maybe it was his chin, which was a small, pink hill in the gentle plain of his face.

While I watched him, he lifted his hand and felt carefully of his nose. Then he saw me. His eyes had that kind of mistiness that seems to go with age or illness, though he wasn't really old or sick, either. He brought his hand down quickly and picked up the pencil, but he saw I still was looking at the nose, and finally he sighed and said, "That Slade."

Just the sound of the name brought Slade to my eye. I saw him slouched in front of the bar, and I saw him and his string coming down the grade from the buttes, the wheel horses held snug and the rest lined out pretty, and then the string leveling off and Slade's whip lifting hair from a horse that wasn't up in the collar. I had heard it said that Slade could make a horse scream with that whip. Slade's name wasn't Freighter, of course. Our town had nicknamed him that because that was what he was.

"I don't think it's any good to send him a bill, Mr. Baumer," I said. "He can't even read."

"He could pay yet."

"He don't pay anybody," I said.

"I think he hate me," Mr. Baumer went on. "That is the thing. He hate me for coming not from this country. I come here, sixteen years old, and learn to read and write, and I make a business, and so I think he hate me."

"He hates everybody."

Mr. Baumer shook his head. "But not to pinch the nose. Not to call Dutchie."

The side door squeaked open, but it was only Colly Coleman coming in from a trip so I said, "Excuse me, Mr. Baumer, but you shouldn't have trusted him in the first place."

"I know," he answered, looking at me with his misty eyes. "A man make mistakes. I think some do not trust him, so he will pay me because I do. And I do not know him well then. He only came back to town three-four months ago, from being away since before I go into business."

"People who knew him before could have told you," I said.

"A man make mistakes," he explained again.

"It's not my business, Mr. Baumer, but I would forget the bill."

His eyes rested on my face for a long minute, as if they didn't see me but the problem itself. He said, "It is not twenty-vun dollars and fifty cents now, Al. It is not that any more."

"What is it?"

He took a little time to answer. Then he brought his two hands up as if to help him shape the words. "It is the thing. You see, it is the thing."

I wasn't quite sure what he meant.

He took his pencil from behind the ear where he had put it and studied the point of it. "That Slade. He steal whisky and call it evaporation. He sneak things from his load. A thief, he is. And too big for me."

I said, "I got no time for him, Mr. Baumer, but I guess there never was a freighter didn't steal whisky. That's what I hear."

It was true, too. From the railroad to Moon Dance was fifty miles and a little better—a two-day haul in good weather, heck knew how long in bad. Any freight string bound home with a load had to lie out at least one night. When a freighter had his stock tended to and maybe a little fire going against the dark, he'd tackle a barrel of whisky or of grain alcohol if he had one aboard, consigned to Hirsch Brothers or Mr. Baumer's or the Moon Dance Saloon or the Gold Leaf Bar. He'd drive a hoop out of place, bore a little hole with a nail or bit and draw off what he wanted. Then he'd plug the hole with a whittled peg and pound the hoop back. That was evaporation. Nobody complained much. With freighters you generally took what they gave you, within reason.

"Moore steals it, too," I told Mr. Baumer. Moore was Mr. Baumer's freighter.

"Yah," he said, and that was all, but I stood there for a minute, thinking there might be something more. I could see thought swimming in his eyes, above that little hill of chin. Then a customer came in, and I had to go wait on him.

Nothing happened for a month, nothing between Mr. Baumer and Slade, that is, but fall drew on toward winter and the first flight of ducks headed south and Mr. Baumer hired Miss Lizzie Webb to help with the just-beginning Christmas trade, and here it was, the first week in October, and he and I walked up the street again with the monthly bills. He always sent them out. I guess he had to. A bigger store, like Hirsch's, would wait on the ranchers until their beef or wool went to market.

Up to a point things looked and happened almost the same as they had before, so much the same that I had the crazy feeling I was going through that time again. There was a wagon and a rig tied up at Hirsch's rack and a saddle horse standing hipshot in front of the harness shop. A few more people were on the street now, not many, and lamps had been lit against the shortened day.

It was dark enough that I didn't make out Slade right away. He was just a figure that came out of the yellow wash of light from the Moon Dance Saloon and stood on the board walk and with his head made the little motion of spitting. Then I recognized the lean, raw shape of him and the muscles flowing down into the sloped shoulders, and in the settling darkness I filled the picture in—the dark skin and the flat cheeks and the peevish eyes and the mustache growing rank.

There was Slade and here was Mr. Baumer with his bills and here I was, just as before, just like in the second go-round of a bad dream. I felt like turning back, being embarrassed and half scared by trouble even when it wasn't mine. Please, I said to myself, don't stop, Mr. Baumer! Don't bite off anything! Please, shortsighted the way you are, don't catch sight of him at all! I held up and stepped around behind Mr. Baumer and came up on the outside so as to be between him and Slade where maybe I'd cut off his view.

But it wasn't any use. All along I think I knew it was no use, not the praying or the walking between or anything. The act had to play itself out.

Mr. Baumer looked across the front of me and saw Slade and hesitated in his step and came to a stop. Then in his slow, business way, his chin held firm against his mouth, he began fingering through the bills, squinting to make out the names. Slade had turned and was watching him, munching on a cud of tobacco like a bull waiting.

"You look, Al," Mr. Baumer said without lifting his face from the bills. "I cannot see so good."

So I looked, and while I was looking Slade must have moved. The next I knew Mr. Baumer was staggering ahead, the envelopes spilling out of his hands. There had been a thump, the clap of a heavy hand swung hard on his back.

Slade said, "Haryu, Dutchie?"

Mr. Baumer caught his balance and turned around, the

bills he had trampled shining white between them and, at Slade's feet, the hat that Mr. Baumer had stumbled out from under.

Slade picked up the hat and scuffed through the bills and held it out. "Cold to be goin' without a sky-piece," he said.

Mr. Baumer hadn't spoken a word. The lampshine from inside the bar caught his eyes, and in them it seemed to me a light came and went as anger and the uselessness of it took turns in his head.

Two men had come up on us and stood watching. One of them was Angus McDonald, who owned the Ranchers' Bank, and the other was Dr. King. He had his bag in his hand.

Two others were drifting up, but I didn't have time to tell who. The light came in Mr. Baumer's eyes, and he took a step ahead and swung. I could have hit harder myself. The first landed on Slade's cheek without hardly so much as jogging his head, but it let hell loose in the man. I didn't know he could move so fast. He slid in like a practiced fighter and let Mr. Baumer have it full in the face.

Mr. Baumer slammed over on his back, but he wasn't out. He started lifting himself. Slade leaped ahead and brought a boot heel down on the hand he was lifting himself by. I heard meat and bone under that heel and saw Mr. Baumer fall back and try to roll away.

Things had happened so fast that not until then did anyone have a chance to get between them. Now Mr. McDonald pushed at Slade's chest, saying, "That's enough, Freighter. That's enough now," and Dr. King lined up, too, and another man I didn't know, and I took a place, and we formed a kind of screen between them. Dr. King turned and bent to look at Mr. Baumer.

"Damn fool hit me first," Slade said.

"That's enough," Mr. McDonald told him again while Slade looked at all of us as if he'd spit on us for a nickel. Mr. McDonald went on, using a half-friendly tone, and I knew it was because he didn't want to take Slade on any more than the rest of us did. "You go on home and sleep it off, Freighter. That's the ticket."

Slade just snorted.

From behind us Dr. King said, "I think you've broken this man's hand."

"Lucky for him I didn't kill him," Slade answered. "Damn Dutch penny-pincher!" He fingered the chew out of his mouth. "Maybe he'll know enough to leave me alone now."

Dr. King had Mr. Baumer on his feet. "I'll take him to the office," he said.

Blood was draining from Mr. Baumer's nose and rounding the curve of his lip and dripping from the sides of his chin. He held his hurt right hand in the other. But a thing was that he didn't look beaten even then, not the way a man who has given up looks beaten. Maybe that was why Slade said, with a show of that fierce anger, "You stay away from me! Hear? Stay clear away, or you'll get more of the same!"

Dr. King led Mr. Baumer away, Slade went back into the bar, and the other men walked off, talking about the fight. I got down and picked up the bills, because I knew Mr. Baumer would want me to, and mailed them at the post office, dirty as they were. It made me sorer, someway, that Slade's bill was one of the few that wasn't marked up. The cleanness of it seemed to say that there was no getting the best of him.

Mr. Baumer had his hand in a sling the next day and wasn't much good at waiting on the trade. I had to hustle all afternoon and so didn't have a chance to talk to him even if he had wanted to talk. Mostly he stood at his desk, and once, passing it, I saw he was practicing writing with his left hand. His nose and the edges of the cheeks around it were swollen some.

At closing time I said, "Look, Mr. Baumer, I can lay out of school a few days until you kind of get straightened out here."

"No," he answered as if to wave the subject away. "I get somebody else. You go to school. Is good to learn."

I had a half notion to say that learning hadn't helped him with Slade. Instead, I blurted out that I would have the law on Slade.

"The law?" he asked.

"The sheriff or somebody."

"No, Al," he said. "You would not."

I asked why.

"The law, it is not for plain fights," he said. "Shooting? Robbing? Yes, the law come quick. The plain fights, they are too many. They not count enough."

He was right. I said, "Well, I'd do something anyhow."

"Yes," he answered with a slow nod of his head. "Something you vould do, Al." He didn't tell me what.

Within a couple of days he got another man to clerk for him—it was Ed Hempel, who was always finding and losing jobs—and we made out. Mr. Baumer took his hand from the sling in a couple or three weeks, but with the tape on it it still wasn't any use to him. From what you could see of the fingers below the tape it looked as if it never would be.

He spent most of his time at the high desk, sending me or Ed out on the errands he used to run, like posting and getting the mail. Sometimes I wondered if that was because he was afraid of meeting Slade. He could just as well have gone himself. He wasted a lot of hours just looking at nothing, though I will have to say he worked hard at learning to write left-handed.

Then, a month and a half before Christmas, he hired Slade to haul his freight for him.

Ed Hempel told me about the deal when I showed up for work. "Yessir," he said, resting his foot on a crate in the storeroom where we were supposed to be working. "I tell you he's throwed in with Slade. Told me this morning to go out and locate him if I could and bring him in. Slade was at the saloon, o' course, and says to hell with Dutchie, but I told him this was honest-to-God business, like Baumer had told me to, and there was a quart of whisky right there in the store for him if he'd come and get it. He was out of money, I reckon, because the quart fetched him."

"What'd they say?" I asked him.

"Search me. There was two or three people in the store and Baumer told me to wait on 'em, and he and Slade palavered back by the desk."

"How do you know they made a deal?"

Ed spread his hands out. " 'Bout noon, Moore came in with his string, and I heard Baumer say he was makin' a change. Moore didn't like it too good, either."

It was a hard thing to believe, but there one day was Slade with a pile of stuff for the Moon Dance Mercantile

Company, and that was proof enough with something left for boot.

Mr. Baumer never opened the subject up with me, though I gave him plenty of chances. And I didn't feel like asking. He didn't talk much these days but went around absent-minded, feeling now and then of the fingers that curled yellow and stiff out of the bandage like the toes on the leg of a dead chicken. Even on our walks home he kept his thoughts to himself.

I felt different about him now, and was sore inside. Not that I blamed him exactly. A hundred and thirty-five pounds wasn't much to throw against two hundred. And who could tell what Slade would do on a bellyful of whisky? He had promised Mr. Baumer more of the same, hadn't he? But I didn't feel good. I couldn't look up to Mr. Baumer like I used to and still wanted to. I didn't have the beginning of an answer when men cracked jokes or shook their heads in sympathy with Mr. Baumer, saying Slade had made him come to time.

Slade hauled in a load for the store, and another, and Christmas time was drawing on and trade heavy, and the winter that had started early and then pulled back came on again. There was a blizzard and then a still cold and another blizzard and afterwards a sunshine that was ice-shine on the drifted snow. I was glad to be busy, selling overshoes and sheep-lined coats and mitts and socks as thick as saddle blankets and Christmas candy out of buckets and hickory nuts and the fresh oranges that the people in our town never saw except when Santa Claus was coming.

One afternoon when I lit out from class the thermometer on the school porch read 42° below. But you didn't have to look at it to know how cold the weather was.

Your nose and fingers and toes and ears and the bones inside you told you. The snow cried when you stepped on it.

I got to the store and took my things off and scuffed my hands at the stove for a minute so's to get life enough in them to tie a parcel. Mr. Baumer—he was always polite to me—said, "Hello, Al. Not so much to do today. Too cold for customers." He shuddered a little, as if he hadn't got the chill off even yet, and rubbed his broken hand with the good one. "Ve need Christmas goods," he said, looking out the window to the furrows that wheels had made in the snow-banked street, and I knew he was thinking of Slade's string, inbound from the railroad, and the time it might take even Slade to travel those hard miles.

Slade never made it at all.

Less than an hour later our old freighter, Moore, came in, his beard white and stiff with frost. He didn't speak at first but looked around and clumped to the stove and took off his heavy mitts, holding his news inside him.

Then he said, not pleasantly, "Your new man's dead, Baumer."

"My new man?" Mr. Baumer said.

"Who the hell do you think? Slade. He's dead."

All Mr. Baumer could say was, "Dead!"

"Froze to death, I figger," Moore told him while Colly Coleman and Ed Hempel and Miss Lizzie and I and a couple of customers stepped closer.

"Not Slade," Mr. Baumer said. "He know too much to freeze."

"Maybe so, but he sure's God's froze now. I got him in the wagon."

We stood looking at one another and at Moore. Moore

was enjoying his news, enjoying feeding it out bit by bit so's to hold the stage. "Heart might've give out for all I know."

The side door swung open, letting in a cloud of cold and three men who stood, like us, waiting on Moore. I moved a little and looked through the window and saw Slade's freight outfit tied outside with more men around it. Two of them were on a wheel of one of the wagons, looking inside.

"Had a extra man, so I brought your stuff in," Moore went on. "Figgered you'd be glad to pay for it."

"Not Slade," Mr. Baumer said again.

"You can take a look at him."

Mr. Baumer answered no.

"Someone's takin' word to Connor to bring his hearse. Anyhow I told 'em to. I carted old Slade this far. Connor can have him now."

Moore pulled on his mitts. "Found him there by the Deep Creek crossin', doubled up in the snow an' his fire out." He moved toward the door. "I'll see to the horses, but your stuff'll have to set there. I got more'n enough work to do at Hirsch's."

Mr. Baumer just nodded.

I put on my coat and went out and waited my turn and climbed on a wagon wheel and looked inside, and there was Slade piled on some bags of bran. Maybe because of being frozen, his face was whiter than I ever saw it, whiter and deader, too, though it never had been lively. Only the mustache seemed still alive, sprouting thick like greasewood from alkali. Slade was doubled up all right, as if he had died and stiffened leaning forward in a chair.

I got down from the wheel, and Colly and then Ed

climbed up. Moore was unhitching, tossing off his pieces
of information while he did so. Pretty soon Mr. Connor
came up with his old hearse, and he and Moore tumbled
Slade into it, and the team that was as old as the hearse
made off, the tires squeaking in the snow. The people
trailed on away with it, their breaths leaving little rib-
bons of mist in the air. It was beginning to get dark.

Mr. Baumer came out of the side door of the store,
bundled up, and called to Colly and Ed and me. "We
unload," he said. "Already is late. Al, better you get a
couple lanterns now."

We did a fast job, setting the stuff out of the wagons
on to the platform and then carrying it or rolling it on
the one truck that the store owned and stowing it inside
according to where Mr. Baumer's good hand pointed.

A barrel was one of the last things to go in. I edged it
up and Colly nosed the truck under it, and then I let it
fall back. "Mr. Baumer," I said, "we'll never sell all
this, will we?"

"Yah," he answered. "Sure we sell it. I get it cheap. A
bargain, Al, so I buy it."

I looked at the barrel head again. There in big letters
I saw WOOD ALCOHOL—DEADLY POISON.

"Hurry now," Mr. Baumer said. "Is late." For a flash
and no longer I saw through the mist in his eyes, saw,
you might say, that hilly chin repeated there. "Then ve
go home, Al. Is good to know to read."

FIRST
PRINCIPAL

THE FIRST MAN Lonnie Ellenwood saw to remember after the stage arrived at Moon Dance was Mr. Ross, the chairman of the school board.

The second was the man with the yellow eyes.

The first one stepped out and stood by the wheel as the driver checked the horses. His voice boomed up at Lonnie's father before they could get down. "Howdy there, Professor. I'm Ross. Glad to see you."

The man stood as high as a high-headed horse. He had a red face and bright blue eyes. "Howdy, Mrs. Ellenwood. How's Ohio?" He offered a hand to match the voice. "Hope you're going to like it here."

He stooped to shake hands with Lonnie. "Howdy there. Guess you're too young for your dad's new high school. Like to fish, Bub?" Lonnie smelled the evil smell of whisky on his breath. The man straightened and turned to Mr. Ellenwood. "We can go, soon's we get your plunder."

They stood in front of a frame hotel—Lonnie and his parents and Mr. Ross in a little group—and the grown people talked while they waited for the driver to hand down the baggage. A sign across the hotel said HERREN HOUSE. Another, below it, said BAR. The other buildings along the street were wooden, too, and mostly one-story. The dust that the stage had raised was settling back.

A line of men leaned against the front of the hotel, watching from under wide hats. Lonnie saw curiosity in their faces, and doubt and maybe dislike for the new principal and his wife and boy. At first he thought the men all looked alike—weathered cheeks, blue or black shirts, faded pants—and then he saw the man with the yellow eyes. They weren't exactly yellow, though, but pale brown, pale enough to look yellow, yellow and cold like a cat's. Under his nose was a cat's draggle of mustache.

The eyes caught Lonnie's and held them, and Lonnie felt a quick alarm, seeing bold and rude in them the veiled suspicions of the rest.

"Kind of raw country to you, I guess, Prof," Mr. Ross was saying, "but you'll get along." He took a cigar from the pocket of his unbuttoned vest and bit the end off it and spit it out. "Great country, Montana is, and bound to be better. We got a church already, like I told you in my letter, and now we'll have a high school. Yep, you'll get along."

Two of the men who lounged against the hotel were chewing tobacco, staining the plank sidewalk with thoughtful spurts of spit. A swinging door divided them, and a sweet-sour smell came from inside.

"Preacher's a fine man, or so they tell me," Mr. Ross went on. "He figured to be here, only a funeral came up."

Beside Mr. Ross, beside the shirt sleeves and the open vest, Mr. Ellenwood looked small and pale, and too proper in the new suit he'd bought in Cincinnati.

Lonnie's mother wasn't paying any attention to the watching men. She looked up and down the dusty street, at the board buildings that fronted up to it, and at the sky that arched over. She smiled down at Lonnie and touched him on the shoulder. "This is our new home, son."

He didn't answer. He wished he were back in Ohio, screened in the friendly woods and hills, away from this bare, flat land where even the sun seemed to stare at him.

Mr. Ross was still talking. "I got a team hitched around the corner. I'll ride you over. Hope you like the house we got for you."

The stage driver had set the baggage down. Mr. Ross grabbed hold of a bag and suitcase and an old telescope and began walking along with Mrs. Ellenwood.

As Lonnie's father started to follow, carrying a box in one hand and a straw suitcase in the other, a man lurched from the door of the hotel and fell against him and caught his balance and went swaying up the street talking to himself.

When Lonnie brought his gaze back from the man, he saw his father leaning over. The suitcase had broken open and spilled towels and cold cream and powder and one of his mother's petticoats on the walk. Father was stuffing them back in, stuffing them in slowly one by one while blood colored his neck.

The men were laughing, not very loud but inside themselves while they tried to keep their mouths straight. Only the man with the yellow eyes really let his laughs come out. He was angled against the wall of the hotel, one booted foot laid across the other. His voice sounded in little jeering explosions.

Mr. Ellenwood didn't say anything. He went ahead

stuffing things back into the suitcase and trying to make the lock catch afterwards.

Mr. Ross looked back and saw what had happened and turned around and returned. His face got redder than ever. To the one man he said, "Funny, ain't it, Chilter!"

"To me it is," the man answered and laughed again.

Mrs. Ellenwood was standing where Mr. Ross had left her. Lonnie saw an anxious look on her face.

Mr. Ellenwood finally got the lock to catch. He picked up the suitcase, and they started off again, the eyes following them and then being lost around a corner. Mr. Ross didn't speak until they had put the baggage in the buggy, and then all he said was, "Sorry, Prof."

Lonnie's father sat quietly while Mr. Ross cramped the wheel around and got straightened out. "It's all right." His voice was even. "It doesn't matter."

Mrs. Ellenwood smiled at Lonnie. "I guess it was funny, to everybody but us."

Mr. Ross grunted as if he didn't think so.

He came around the next day, the day before school was to open. "Like I told you," he promised Mr. Ellenwood, "next year we'll have a building, but the old hall'll have to do until then. You seen it? Everything shipshape?" He stood half a foot higher than Mr. Ellenwood. He was bigger, thicker, stronger, more assured. When he laughed he rattled the china that Lonnie's mother hadn't found a place for yet. He turned to Lonnie. "Your school don't start till next week, eh, Bub?"

He bit off the end of a cigar and lighted up and settled back in the rocking chair. "You're going to like it here, Prof. It ain't much, in a way, but in a way it is, too.

Best damn people—excuse me—that ever lived, most of 'em. You'll see."

Mr. Ellenwood was nodding politely.

"Kind of rough, but you'll get on."

"Yes," Mr. Ellenwood said and waited for Mr. Ross to say more.

Mr. Ross took his cigar out and rolled it between his fingers. He studied it for a long time. "People'll take to you," he said slowly as if reading the words from the cigar, "soon as they learn you ain't being buffaloed."

"I don't know that I know what you mean."

"It's just a word, is all. Comes, I guess, because buffalo scare kind of easy."

"I see."

Mr. Ross squirmed in the rocker. He rolled the cigar some more, and then chewed on it and pulled and let out a plume of smoke. "Some maybe ain't used to a man teaching school," he said, not looking at Mr. Ellenwood.

"I see."

"You'll get on. Mostly it's women who teach in this country."

"I see."

Mrs. Ellenwood came from the kitchen. She said good morning.

Mr. Ross lifted himself from the rocker. "Howdy, ma'am. Preacher been around yet, and Mrs. Rozzell?"

Mrs. Ellenwood nodded. "Yesterday."

"We liked them," Mr. Ellenwood said.

Lonnie's mother put her hand on his father's shoulder. "They insist Tom has to be superintendent of the Sunday school."

Mr. Ross nodded and smoked some more on his cigar.

When he got up to go, Mr. Ellenwood stepped to the door with him. "We'll get on, as you say."

For what seemed a long time, Mr. Ross looked him up and down. Lonnie wondered if he saw a kind of chunky man, not very tall, with a pale complexion and sandy hair and the look of books and church about him, a man firm in the right but not forward, not hearty and sure like Mr. Ross himself.

"O' course," Mr. Ross said, "you'll get on." He put his cigar back in his mouth and closed the door.

It rained the next day, a cold misty rain that sifted out of the north. The air was still wet with drizzle that afternoon as Lonnie started out to meet his father on his return from school. The dirt trails that passed for streets were sticky with mud. At the crossings Lonnie hopped and skipped until he reached the plank sidewalk again, but even so he got mud on his shoes.

A little bunch of cattle was being herded down the street. Lonnie could see the horseman behind them, reining to and fro to bring up the poky ones and flicking at them with his quirt. The cattle had their heads stuck out, their eyes big with the strangeness of town, their mouths opening to a lost mooing. The voice of the driver as he herded them along came to Lonnie like a snarl.

For a minute he was frightened, seeing the cattle coming his way and the long horns gleaming white, and then he saw his father and felt safe and hurried along to meet him. Mr. Ellenwood was walking with half a dozen boys and girls. They were students, Lonnie guessed. He saw his father lift his head and turn his face toward the horseman. The boys and girls stopped. The rider pulled up, held his horse for a moment, and then reined over.

Lonnie had got close enough to hear. The rider said, "How was that, schoolteacher?"

Even before he saw for sure, Lonnie felt his insides tighten. The man was Chilter of the almost yellow eyes and the cat's mustache beneath.

"I asked you to stop that cursing."

Chilter spit, then asked, "Why so?"

Mr. Ellenwood made a little motion toward the boys and girls. "You can see why."

For a while the man didn't say anything. He sat his horse, curbing it as it tried to step around, and let his gaze go over Mr. Ellenwood. He looked big, sitting there over everybody. "Why," he said, "I heard this was a free country."

Mr. Ellenwood stepped out into the mud. He didn't speak; he just stepped out into the mud, his face lifted and his gaze steady.

The cat eyes looked him over. They traveled down the street to the cattle. Lonnie saw that the bunch was loosening. Some had poked through the open gate of a front yard. Some had started up an alley. A man came out of a door and called from the front yard. "Hey, you, haze these steers away, will you?"

Mr. Ellenwood said, "These are just children."

The eyes came back to him. They looked him over again, slowly, yellow and cold and scornful. The man spit and dug his spurs into his horse. It threw some mud on Mr. Ellenwood as it lunged. When it had run a little way, Chilter jerked it up and turned in his saddle and lifted his hat and bobbed his head at Mr. Ellenwood as if speaking to a lady.

Mr. Ellenwood pulled back from the mud. He kept silent, walking home, even after the high-schoolers had dropped away one by one. Lonnie wanted to question him but felt closed off. And when finally the words came to his mouth, he would see the man turning and lifting his hat, like saying, "Excuse me, ma'am," and anger or shame or the fear in his stomach kept them unsaid. All he managed was, "Mother said to tell you she was meeting with the ladies of the church."

At home Mr. Ellenwood changed clothes and went out into the back yard and began to split wood for the kitchen range. Lonnie sat on the steps and watched.

It had quit drizzling. In the west the sun showed red through black clouds. The sharp smell of fall was in the air, the smell of summer done and things dying, of cold to come, of leaves that someone was trying to make into a bonfire.

Lonnie's father was still chopping wood when Mr. Ross came clattering down the back steps. "Couldn't rouse anyone," Mr. Ross explained, "so I come on through, figuring you might be out here in back."

Mr. Ellenwood anchored the axe in the chopping block and turned to talk.

Mr. Ross bobbed his head toward Lonnie, and Mr. Ellenwood said, "You run in the house, son."

Lonnie backed up and lagged up the steps, but he didn't go in. He sat down on the porch, behind the low wall of it, and listened and now and then dared a look.

"Might as well tell you, Prof," Mr. Ross said, "that man Chilter's up to the saloon, making big medicine against you."

Mr. Ellenwood nodded, as if he expected it all the time.

"I don't know what to tell you."

"Nothing. It's all right."

"He's got a kind of a reputation as a bad actor."

"Oh."

"You got a gun or something?"

"I wouldn't want a gun."

"No?"

"No."

"You can't just hold quiet, and let him do whatever he figures on!"

"I'll just have to wait and see."

"I could stay with you, I guess." It was as if the words were being pulled out of Mr. Ross.

Mr. Ellenwood looked him in the eye. "Mr. Ross," he said, "a man has to hoe his own row, here or in Ohio."

"Good for you. I wasn't so sure about Ohio. I kind of wish you'd let me give you a six-shooter. I brought one along for you, just in case."

"No. Thanks."

"He ain't likely to use one. More likely to be fist fighting or wrastling, no holds barred."

"Anyhow, you go on."

"I might hang around, kind of out of sight."

"You go on."

Mr. Ross rolled his lower lip with his thumb and forefinger. "Damn if I ain't acting like a mother hen." He laughed without humor. "Good luck, Prof." He turned and walked away. Lonnie could see, before he rounded the corner of the house, that his face was troubled.

Later, out of the beginning dusk, the man came riding. Far off, before he could see him, Lonnie heard the quick suck of horse's hoofs in the mud. They might have been meaningless at first, just sounds that went along with other sounds like the creak of an axle and the cry of children and the whisper of wind, except that already

Lonnie knew, and his stomach sickened and the blood raced in him.

He wanted to cry out, wanted to shout the man was coming, wanted to scream that here he was, forever identifiable now by the mere turn of a shoulder and the set of his head.

The man didn't speak. He just kept coming, his horse's feet dancing fancy in the mud.

Mr. Ellenwood raised his axe and saw him and tapped the axehead into the block and stood straight.

The man rode from the alley into the unfenced back yard, and for a minute Lonnie thought he meant to ride his father down. Then he saw the hand leap up and the butt of the quirt arching from it. The quirt came down to the sound of torn air.

A weal sprang out on Mr. Ellenwood's face. One second it wasn't there, and the next it was, like something magical, a red and purple weal swollen high as half a rope. It ran from the temple across the cheek and down the line of the jaw.

For one breath it was like looking at a picture, the horse pulled up, the quirt downswept from the hand, the weal hot and angry, and nothing moving, everything caught up and held by the violence that had gone before.

The picture broke into sound and fury, father's hand shooting out and catching the man's arm and tearing him from his horse and the horse snorting and shying away and the man landing sprawled and gathering himself like a cat and raising the quirt high again while swear words streamed from his mouth.

Mr. Ellenwood was stepping, stepping forward, not back, stepping into the wicked whistle and cut of the quirt, his head up and his eyes fixed. There was a ter-

rible rightness about him, a rightness so terrible and so
fated that for a minute Lonnie couldn't bear to look,
thinking of Stephen stoned and Christ dying on the cross
—of all the pale, good, thoughtful men foredoomed before the hearty.

He heard the whine of the quirt and the two men
grunting and the whine of the quirt and feet slipping in
the wet grass and breaths hoarse in the throat and the
sound of the quirt again.

He heard the grunting and the slipping and the hoarse
breathing, and all at once he remembered he didn't
hear the quirt now, and he looked and saw it looping
away, thrown by his father's hand. He saw his father's
fists begin to work and heard the flat smacks of bone
against flesh and saw the man try to shield himself and
go down and get up and go down again. His eyes ran
from side to side like a cornered animal's. He began
crawling away. Rather than meet those fists again, he
crawled away, beaten and silent, and climbed his horse
and rode off.

Mr. Ellenwood watched him, then turned and saw
Lonnie, who had come off the porch and down the steps.
"Son," he said sternly, still panting, "I thought I told
you to go inside."

From a distance Mr. Ross's voice, raised in a great
whoop, came to Lonnie's ears.

"I did—I mean I couldn't. I just couldn't."

Lonnie watched his father's face, wanting, now that
he had won, to see it loosen and light up and the weal
bend to a smile.

"You're pale as paper, son."

"I didn't know if you could fight. I didn't know if you
would think it was right to fight."

Mr. Ross's voice drowned out the answer. From across the street it boomed at them, the words sounding almost like hurrahs. "By God, Prof, you're all right!"

Mr. Ellenwood straightened and turned in the direction of the voice, and then turned back and looked at Lonnie and abruptly sat down on the step by him. "If a man has to fight, he has to fight, Lonnie."

Mr. Ross came marching through the mud, his big mouth open in a smile. "I saw it, Prof. I hung around. Damn me, if that ain't a bridge crossed!" He stuck out his hand.

Mr. Ellenwood took the hand and answered, "Thanks," but he didn't smile back. He looked at Mr. Ross and then looked off into space.

Mr. Ross said, "There's one man ain't going to be thinking education's so sissified."

Father nodded at the space he was looking into. "One," he said.

LAST SNAKE

~~~~~~

THE NOISES of the night kept Ross awake. He lay under his bush and listened, his mind building things out of the sounds that he couldn't place.

There was the lipping of the Missouri along its banks, the rush and mutter of the current, the whine of the west wind in the trees that rose darkly above him, the far howling of wolves. These he could account for. But the crackling of a twig, the give of the willows, as if brushed by skin or fur, by Pawnees or Sioux or Rees or the great fierce bear that mountain men told about! He saw them in the dark—Pawnees with roached combs of hair and painted faces, the white bear smelling him out, its jaws dripping. They made Carpentier seem tame. Almost, he would have welcomed Carpentier.

He lay tense under the bush, needled with alarms, feeling danger closing in, feeling the great lost distances of the Missouri pressing him, seeing the days ahead in a long parade of frights and fatigue and hunger. A coyote yipped close, and he pictured Indians making animal noises as they crept ahead with their scalping knives, and fright threaded through him, running along with his blood.

He had given in to fear. It had seeped into him day by

day as the keelboat fought the mad Missouri and the gentle hills and woods of home had run out into bald, deserted deeps of land and sky. He had given in to fear and felt no shame about it. It left no room for shame. He had to get away, away from the dreadful distances, away from even dreader things ahead, back to St. Charles or St. Louis or the farm he'd left, where trees and houses arose round a man and, if he liked, at night he could hear the give-and-take over glasses in taverns.

Through his bush he could see a handful of stars, shining far off and lonely, paling to the upcoming moon. He wished for morning to come so that he could see, so that he could be on his way, hard though it was, through thickets and trees and deadfall along the river. Along the bare hills the going would be easier, except that Indians might spot him and cut his scalp away.

The cold of earth was creeping into his clothes, inside the worn breeches, inside the coat, into his smallclothes, inside the skin itself, so that he knew how it was with a snake.

His Pap had said you had to kill your own snakes, and Pap had killed his, except at the last. A strong, mean, bossy man, Pap had been, saying, "Maul them rails today. Hear!" or "Git the field planted" or "I'll whop hell out of ye, boy, if'n you don't git off your backside!"

He could listen for noises and be afraid and think about Pap all at the same time, as if part of him was here and part of him back there, hating Pap again, seeing the bushed face and the little eyes and the hand ready with a whip. Nothing had fazed Pap, not nature or man or anything until the last. He had stood strong, sure of himself, bossing his family and fighting neighbors if need be. In a way, you had to give him credit.

The wind had lulled to a whisper, and now it was gone. Ross thought he heard something—movements off at the edge of hearing, the rumble of voices, a step and silence and a step, and the water quiet now along the shore, and somewhere a bird cried and he caught the whistle of wings. It was a breeze playing tricks in the bushes; it was his ears overstraining; it was just that he was beat down and nervous. He waited, his breath light in his throat, but the sounds didn't come again, and he didn't know whether it was worse or better not to hear them.

At the last, Pap had weakened, and it had come to Ross with a sick jolt that some things were too much even for him. Pap with the bellyache, the long bellyache, and the strong voice whiny, and the little eyes looking for the help he'd never asked before. Pap feeling sorry for himself, saying, "God, can't you help a man?" or "I'm tarnally sick, Andy," or "Seems like I'm too young to die. I don't care to die." His bushed face would twist and his eyes leak tears, and he would pray and pray and hold his belly while the strength ran out of him. At the last, Pap couldn't kill his own snakes.

Ross strained for the echo of voices, for the faint step, for the sounds of moving, while the far-off part of him dug at Pap. It was strange he should be thinking so much of Pap, except maybe because Carpentier put him in mind of him. It was while Pap was dying that Ross had hated him most, seeing him turn soft as mush and ask help and want the kindness, the good-wishing he never had given anybody himself. Pap had been like a tree broken down, like a big sycamore or poplar that you would figure should have stood as long as time. Ross wasn't more than twelve, maybe, when Pap turned up his toes, but he had learned something. He hadn't thought the same since. "Maul them rails! Git the crop in!" And then the whiny voice: "Can't you do somep'n for me? You aim just to let me die?"

The night seemed quieter. The stream kept busy and now and then the breeze worked in the trees and the coyote kept yipping, as if to show he was a sure-enough coyote, but the other sounds were gone. Still with his ears cocked, Ross felt himself drifting toward sleep.

He'd have to sleep and be up and away, for they would hunt for him. They would send Carpentier and maybe a man with him, and Carpentier, the woodsman, would follow his trail like a turnpike. Carpentier—with a nose like half a cob and eyes sharp and black as pokeberries, his shoulders wide, his hands hard, but his feet quiet along the banks and his finger clever on the trigger. Carpentier would whip him or shoot him, depending, and take him back to the keelboat, shaken and ashamed inside. It wasn't a little thing, the way they figured, to desert a keelboat bound for the upper Missouri. Men had been killed for it.

It was when he signed up for the trip that he had made his mistake. It was when he agreed to go to Fort Floyd and beyond and had signed his name to a piece of paper. In St. Louis, things seemed exciting upriver. You took a drink or two, and voices joked with you, and you signed up, feeling big.

Afterwards, you learned what you'd done. The pushpole ground into your shoulder, and the towrope, the cordelle, burned in your hand, and you had to unload so as to lighten the boat and float her off bars, and along the deep banks you grabbed at brush and pulled her along. And you tried to keep up with the Creoles, who could work from before sunup to after sundown, and then sing a song and catch a piece of sleep and be ready to go again.

It wasn't the work, though, that bothered him; all his life he had worked. It was that the country got wilder every day, the river lonelier, the trees scantier, until at last the great bald hills ran out from the river, ran on forever, to distances that numbed the mind.

Lying there close to sleep, he knew it was the emptiness, the lostness that scared him most and swelled his other fears. He was a woodsman, a hill-and-tree and closed-in man. Out where the sky lifted and the trees runted away and the eye ran dizzy, he saw the roached Indians forming out of nothing, the white bear rising from the empty land, and death laughing in the open waters and along the straggly shores.

"Poltron!" Carpentier had called him, his broad face snarling. "Coward!"—because once at dusk, with the sun sunk in fire and loneliness like an ache on the land, he hadn't wanted to take the towrope through a willow thicket. The Creoles were uneasy, too, for they had seen Indians earlier in the day—a dozen Indians who sat their horses on a hill, outlined against the sky, and watched the boat toil up the river. The big eyes of the Creoles swam along the shore to the thicket and back to Carpentier. They were afraid, but they would go, being more afraid of Carpentier, as if he was Pap to all of them.

"I don't care for it," Ross said.

They had brought the keelboat in to the bank, for the water had grown too deep for poles and the wind wrong for the sail, and the crew had piled out. "I don't aim to go," Ross had said.

It was then that Carpentier snarled, "Poltron!" He

made for Ross, his black eyes snapping, while the crew drew back, and he slapped Ross with a hand big as a pie plate and hard as hickory. "Go!"

There was no help for it then, even if Ross had been afraid, and he wasn't afraid exactly, not of Carpentier or of a fight or of things in the open. He had stood up to Pap once, knowing beforehand he would be whipped. He swung, aiming for the half-cob of nose, and Carpentier pulled away from the blow and grinned, liking to fight and finding few to fight with.

Ross rushed and swung again, and felt Carpentier's fist like a club in his face. He covered with his forearm and hit out and heard the knock of bone on bone and felt a numbness in his hand. Far off there came to him a clucking from among the crew, and he knew it was because he had scored.

He bulled at Carpentier, swinging wild, taking blows in return. He screeched out, *"Poltron—"* and caught his toe on a stub. It was only the beginning of Carpentier's lick that he felt.

He came to with an ache in his head and the taste of blood in his mouth. He rolled over and got up, dizzy and silent, and took the rope. The fight was out of him. He reckoned he wasn't born to be a fighter, remembering how Pap had beat him to his will. A silent hate filled him as he and the crew pulled safely through the thicket —hate of himself and of Carpentier and of a world in which he was no better than a bound boy.

It seemed a long time ago, lying under the bush half asleep. He wasn't a talking man, and he hadn't talked to anyone afterwards, except for a word or so with little Nedeau. Nedeau was a splinter of a Frenchman whose eyes spoke the fright in him. "It is too bad, my frien'," he said. "But for the tripping—who knows?—maybe so you would have won."

The sympathy of this small woman of a man half comforted and half shamed Ross. "Wouldn't have made any difference."

"How?"

"We would go on just the same."

"To be sure."

"Doin' this, doin' that, all on somebody else's say-so."

Nedeau's eyes were like a squaw's, large and liquid. He clucked his sympathy.

"I'll get away. I swear I'll get away."

"It would be good, except for Carpentier."

"Damn Carpentier! You up to it?"

The big eyes rolled and he said, "That Carpentier!"

"Keep your mouth shut then."

Nedeau drew back, hurt. He said, "To be sure," and sidled away.

Ross knew then he would run off. He would get up at night while they slept on shore and pick his way among the men and dodge the guard and start downriver.

Was it only last night? The moon tilting up in the east, throwing the shadow of the eastern woods long on the water, the men lying like beasts, like cows in a dark barnyard, a nighthawk's whimper in the deeps overhead, the guard asleep, slumped half off the bole of the tree he had rested his back against . . .

Ross had closed his hand on the rifle by his side. Already he had powder and ball and flint and steel, and in his shot pouch there was the little bit of parched corn he had sneaked from the cook's supplies. He slipped the horn and pouch over his head, working with quick carefulness. Under the rising moon he could make out Carpentier, sleeping five strides away, his back turned, the breath gargling out of his big lungs. The keelboat was a black oval against the running silver of the river. He would sneak to the dead fire and steal a joint of meat, or a piece of the salt pork and a hatful of the lyed corn they had lived on before game grew plenty.

He eased out of his blankets, wondering whether to crawl or walk. To crawl would be less noticeable, but to be caught crawling would be bad. Standing, his rifle would show. A man roused at night didn't take a rifle with him to the skirts of the camp—or powder and ball. He walked stooped over, his rifle held low in his hand.

Carpentier's snore broke off, and Ross halted, feeling the tapping of his heart. He looked around and saw Carpentier move in bed, easing himself on the ground. The snoring began again, short and light at first, then long and deep. Ross let a foot move, and the other, making toward the dead fire. The cook slept flat on his back, his face open to the night. The moonlight glinted on the ball of an eye not quite shut. Ross held up again, watching the eye. It seemed to him that the night under the moon was light as day, except in the crouching shadows of the trees.

The cook had put his supplies away, packed them away in great round cans that were proof against rats and mice. The cans had lids that came off hard. He tried one of them and gave up, knowing it would make a noise as his nails pulled it free. The kettle sat black in the white ash of the burned fire. He reached toward it, slowly, and remembered that it held a stew; he couldn't carry a stew in his hands.

As he stooped, uncertain, the guard grunted and hitched himself back against the tree. He would be half awake now, making his sleepy eyes find the keelboat, making them search the edges of darkness, making them travel over the camp, before he let himself drop off again. If he called, Ross would say, "I'm hungry."

He waited for the call, his rifle flat against the ground. He made himself hold still and breathe light. The guard began to sag over.

Of a sudden, Ross gave up the idea of food. He felt a panic rising in him. He must get away. He must slide in the cover of the trees. He slowed his panic to a soft pace. The shadows eased toward him, the cottonwoods and willows. They took him in.

He halted in the darkness, torn now inside, wanting to go back and wake Nedeau and beckon him to come. Now that he was away, about to be lost in this wild and end- less world, he thought he couldn't stand up to it alone. But Nedeau wouldn't come. Or he would make a noise. He would cry out at being touched—the sudden, hoarse cry of a man sleeping with fear.

The river glimmered through the trees. Ross got his bearings and started off again, trying to walk quietly like Carpentier, like a wild thing, like an Indian.

He walked all night, while fears crested in him and died away and crested again. An elk or deer rustled up ahead of him and crashed through the brush. A fowl—a wild goose, he guessed it was—broke from under his feet as he walked along the shore. He heard sounds, of skunk or rabbit or the moccasined feet of Indians. He walked far into the day, knowing the hunt was on, that some- where behind him came Carpentier, reading the signs of his passing as another man might read a page of print. He held to the fringe of growth in the valley, squirming through willows, climbing over deadfall and drift, sometimes sighting the bare ridges that lifted beyond the valley floor and wishing he might travel there. But Carpentier would spot him—and Indians, the blood-hungry Rees or Pawnees or Sioux who invaded the country of the harmless Poncas.

He had stopped on a tongue of land that lifted from the river and found the bush he lay under now and crawled beneath it, his legs limber, his stomach empty, the corn long since eaten.

Sleep teased away from him. He thought he heard a step again, and again he wanted to rush out. It was the not knowing that undid him. It was the thinking ahead. *Poltron?* He could face what he had to face when he faced it, but not before. Unknown things! Unseen. Fearsome. The awful distance. The white bear creeping on him. Indians gathering around.

He heard only the river and the breeze and tried to shake thought from his head, and after a while he dozed and awakened with the ache of cold in his legs and saw the moon paling in the west and the faint banner of the sun along the eastern hills. He dozed again.

A bird woke him up, welcoming the morning. The sun was half up. Steam lifted from the river. He crawled out from under the bush, dragging his rifle with him, and stumbled to his feet and then he lifted one knee and the other, flexing the kinks from them.

The world lay quiet in the long sun. It lay deserted, as if waiting for the hand of man, for plows and mills and joking voices on a levee. A hawk sailed in the sky. Dew beaded the bushes. Downriver, towns would rise, and men and women would be getting out of snug beds, readying for the day. Somewhere upstream was Carpentier, following like a hound—

And then Carpentier stood before him, in the little clearing between his clump of bushes and the heavier growth that rose farther from the shore. Nedeau, the little Frenchman, was at his side.

"All right, Ross." The known voice came soft as something dreamed. "We catch you."

Carpentier stood still, his rifle ready in the crook of his arm, his broad face showing watchfulness and pleasure with himself.

Ross heard his own voice say, "It was you."

"Me?"

"Walking, talking, last night. Sneaking up on me."

"*Non*. We only guessed. Let down the rifle!"

"We just arrive," Nedeau said. "By river. A man stop at camp in the canoe, and Carpentier he borrow 'er. The river catch us up to you."

"Let down the rifle!"

"No one gets away from Carpentier," Nedeau bragged, and Ross knew he was thinking back, thinking he had been smart not to make a break, too.

Carpentier said, "You come now."

"I ain't going back."

"But yes," said Carpentier.

"I ain't a slave."

"*Non. Voyageur. Engagé.*" Carpentier took a step ahead, over a fallen log that separated them.

Back of him the woods moved. Back of him, of a sudden, in the pattern of branch and leaf, Ross saw the roached combs of his fright, the hunting eyes, the painted faces, hanging without bodies as if blooming in the bush. He stiffened and cried out, "Injuns! Back of you! Injuns!"

Nedeau leaped like a doe and fell behind the log, but

Carpentier stood as before. "It is the old trick. Let down the rifle!"

The feathered arrows sounded like flushed birds, like a family of bobwhites kicked from underfoot. Ross saw Carpentier falter ahead, like a man tripping, and then fall and squirm behind the log, the tufted shaft of an arrow sticking from his back.

He ran for the log himself. An arrow flashed by him. He dropped between Carpentier and Nedeau.

Carpentier was sighting along his rifle. Words came out of him in little grunts of command. "Up! Watch! Up, I say! *Non!* No shoot! One at the time."

Out of the tail of his sight, Ross saw the black eye narrow along the barrel and the long rifle leap to the shot. A howl came out of the woods, and another flight of arrows. They whistled overhead or chunked into the log.

The faces had faded from the woods, the roached combs withered from the bushes. Ross saw the leaves moving, the shine of dew on them.

Carpentier had rolled over to reload.

"Watch now! Not too quick!"

Ross couldn't make out what to shoot. There was movement in the brush, a feather showing, a brown patch of leg, an eye like an acorn, movement sliding into movement, movement sliding into leaves and branches, into nothing, and none fixed long enough to get a bead on.

Nedeau made a noise beside him. He had forgotten Nedeau, but in the instant that he gave himself he saw him frozen behind the log, not daring to poke an eye over or bring the rifle up. There was the look of naked terror in his face, the catching look of terror, and Ross jerked his eyes away, wanting only the numbness, the whirl of things seen and heard, the not thinking of what could be while the body answered to Carpentier's commands.

Carpentier worked with his gun. He lay half on his back, so as to have the cover of the log, and cupped his hand around the muzzle and spilled powder into the slanting barrel and took a ball from his mouth and fumbled it in, his face set and sore because his hands worked poor. Ross hadn't thought until then how hard hit he might be.

Ross hunted the woods and still saw nothing and sneaked another look at Carpentier. The butt of the arrow jerked to Carpentier's motions, binding against the flexing muscle, the head of it cutting deep inside him. The butt hit the ground as he leaned back, and he started up, his jaw ridged.

The bead of Ross's rifle hung on living brown. The flintlock bucked in his hands. The puff of the pan clouded his target, but he knew he had hit. He could tell from the punky sound of the ball, from the cry that went up.

He reached over and pulled Nedeau's gun from him and handed him his own. His voice barked, "Load, you! Help out!" Nedeau only looked at him.

Carpentier had got back on his stomach. He had trouble sliding the rifle up. He ground out, "Only four, five, maybe half dozen. Pawnees." His eye leveled along the barrel, but he didn't shoot. "They draw back, to come again, *peut-être*. Maybe try sneak around." His head began going down by little stages, as if the neck didn't have strength to hold it. He let it rest on his arm. "We 'ave time to breathe."

The brush rustled as the Pawnees pulled away. Deeper into the woods, or maybe beyond them on the foot of the river ridge, they went on, howling.

Nedeau tugged at Ross's sleeve. "We go," he whispered, running his eyes from Ross to Carpentier's bent head. "The dugout, she's just back there. We run. Quick!"

"Carpentier?"

Nedeau still whispered. "He die, anyway."

Carpentier rolled his head on his arm so as to see them. His face was pale as the underside of a fish. Except for the eyes, he might have been dead.

Nedeau looked away.

Ross said, "How you, Carpentier?"

"Not dead." He stared at them quietly, reading what was in their minds and nothing showing in his face except what was there before—the hard strength, the driving power, the harsh force that made a man want to beat him down and break him and see the mush underneath.

The arrow slanted tall from his back. A round, smooth arrow, fitted neat with feathers. An arrow to invite the fingers, the hand, the hard grip, and then the sudden pull. And then the face would break, the pokeberry eyes melt, the hard mouth twist with pleading.

"Quick, Ross!"

Nedeau's small hand pulling at him, and his own hand going out, as if by itself, the balls of the fingers feeling the feathered stick, the fingers closing hard, the arm jerking. His voice sounded choked to him. "Got to get that arrow out."

The body flinched, but not the face. The face said, "*Non.* You leave the head."

The shaft hung and let go and pulled out headless, the end wet and red with blood.

Nedeau's hands kept tugging at Ross. "The river! To St. Louis! Quick! It be too late."

It would be easy. They'd sneak down the bank while the Indians figured on a new attack. They'd jump in the dugout and go.

"Come on! *Mon dieu!*"

It was like someone else speaking, someone with an edge to his voice like a knife. "Can't fool with you, Carpentier." The mind went on, making talk. *Can't fool with you, you hear? No need to keep your eyes on me. Can't boss me, Carpentier, not with a berry patch of eyes and a rock for a face. You're scared, Carpentier. Own up to it. No one kills the last snake.*

The face held him, the cob-nose, berry-eyed face.

Why'n't you beg, Carpentier, you that's so hard? Beg, and I can leave you for mush. Why'n't you beg and leave me go?

It was like reading words in the face, words saying Carpentier would lie there, not begging for anything ever, saying he was hard and ungiving, alive or dead.

"Quick! They stop yelling. They come on."

Ross felt his mouth speaking, heard the words come hoarse. "Get up, Carpentier! You can get up."

Nedeau was crying, *"Non!* You are the crazy man, Ross."

"Crawl then! Here. Arm over my shoulder. We'll both crawl. Crawl, damn you, crawl!"

Travel like a worm. Rocks creeping by, willows, the bush slept under, arm like a bar across his neck. Plant corn, boy. Run like a rabbit, Nedeau. Who cares?

A man could stand up now, screened by bushes. He

could lean his rifle against a willow and listen and hear nothing. He could bend over and get hold of Carpentier and, while his eyes filmed and the blood swelled his skull, lift him over a shoulder and take the rifle and stagger down the bank.

Nedeau was in the dugout, ready to cut loose—too ready.

Ross splashed out and rolled Carpentier in the canoe and got in himself. Nedeau cut the rope and pushed her around and dug with the paddle.

Downstream was St. Charles, St. Louis, New Orleans, the settlements of men; upriver the bald hills, the distances, the world opening into nothing.

Nedeau turned his head around, a question in his eyes. Ross stared back at him. He said, "Which way you *think*, damn it?"

THE
MOON DANCE
SKUNK

~~~~~~

THERE WERE five men in the back room of the Moon Dance bar—three ranchers, a hay hand and a cattle buyer —all idled by the rain that was beating outside. They had quit their pinochle game, the cards and chips lying forgotten on the green table, and were listening to old Ray Gibler who'd started on one of his stories.

Then Ray saw me and grinned and held out his big hand. "How, Tenderfoot."

"I'll listen," I said to Ray. I took off my slicker.

"I was just talking. Ought to be making tracks."

One of the ranchers said, "You ain't gonna ride herd on no dudes today."

"My woman's probably on the hunt for me."

"I'll buy a drink," I said.

Ray gave me his wide grin again. It made deep wrinkles in his leathery cheeks. "I don't like to get in the habit of refusin'."

I yelled to the bartender for a round. "What was this about a skunk?"

"Well, I'll tell you—"

Ray doodled the ice in his ditchwater highball with one horny finger. . . .

104

It was Shorty, the sheepherder, had the skunk, and it happened right here, right in this bar, and there was rooms overhead just like now, only you boys wouldn't remember it, being still slick-eared.

Shorty was new to the town then, but it didn't take us long to find he was all sheepherder. Had a fine, steady thirst and a free hand with money. He had been herding for George I. Smith for five-six months when he decided he couldn't stand thirst nor prosperity any longer. He came to town, a sawed-off, humpy feller with a mop of black hair and a habit of talking to himself, like all herders.

He got fired up good the first day and kep' the blaze going maybe a week, while his whiskers stooled out and his clothes got dirtier and dirtier, and a man meeting him was careful to get on the wind side.

He slept all one day under the hitch rack in back of the Moon Dance Mercantile Company, and when he woke up that night he was just as dry as he was broke, which is as dry as a man can get. He tried moochin' drinks, going from one place to another, but he'd run out of credit, too, and all he got was a bad eye and good advice from the men who had his money.

I was right here, on business you might say, that night when Shorty came in and asked if the roof didn't never leak.

Whitey Hanson said, polishing a glass, "It's leaked plenty. I set 'em up for you three or four times. Git out!"

Shorty tried to argue. "My money, you got it."

"Ah-h. Why'n't you git back on the job?"

There was a couple of curly wolves in the bar, along with Whitey and Shorty and me. Anyhow, they figured they was curly. One of them was Rough Red Rourke and the other Stub Behr. Seeing Shorty, they moseyed over. "Ba-a-a," Red said in his ear, loud enough to bust an eardrum.

"Way round 'em!" Stub yelled.

Red grabbed Shorty by the shoulder. "Them pore ewes are missin' you, sweetheart."

Together they ran Shorty limp-legged through the door and pitched him in the street. Shorty got up slow, talking to himself, and dragged off.

Whitey Hanson thought that was good stuff. He said thankee to Red and Stub and poured drinks on the house.

Must have been a couple of hours later—anyhow along toward midnight—when Shorty showed up again, and not alone neither. He had a skunk with him, carrying it along by the tail so it couldn't do business. Old-timers have seen that trick worked many a time in days before saloons got to be hidyholes for spooners. Of course we didn't know the skunk was Shorty's pet.

Red saw him first and a big, drunk smile came on his face. He couldn't see the skunk on account of Shorty was carrying it on the off side. "Hey, Stub," he said, "look what I see." Then he hollered, "Ba-a-a-a!" at Shorty, so loud the roof shook.

He made for Shorty, and Shorty saw him and a look came on his face. He swung the skunk around. "By damn!" he said.

Red stopped like he'd been butted by a bull. Stub was trying to slip out of sight.

"Way round 'em!" Shorty said, and pointed the skunk and held it low, so's its front feet almost touched the floor. "Git out, both you! Git!"

He hazed them around towards the door, still holding

the skunk low, business end to. It takes an awful brave man to face up to a skunk. Red and Stub wasn't that curly. They got.

Shorty closed the door after them and headed for the bar like a trout for a hopper. This was the business he had come for. He held the skunk up. To Whitey he said, "Set 'em up or I set 'im down!"

"Sure, Shorty, sure. Don't set 'im down. Nice work, Shorty." Whitey came from behind the bar and stretched his arm away out and shook Shorty's loose fist. "Them fellers couldn't buffalo you, Shorty."

Some of the rest of us ambled up, not too close, and told Shorty he sure did shine. Shorty said, "Wasn't nothin'. Wasn't nothin'."

"It sure was, Shorty. Sure was."

I reckon all that glory was too much for Shorty. He wasn't used to compliments, but just to hearing sheep bleat and bartenders say Hell, no, they wouldn't trust him for a drink and why didn't he go to work. Yep, it must have been too much for him. Anyhow, he dropped the skunk.

Whitey jumped the counter like an antelope and tore out the back. Tubby Adams got squoze so hard in the doorway he swore his pants wouldn't fit for a month, being way big in the waist and way short in the leg. It must have taken us all of five seconds to clear out, leaving Shorty and his skunk in the saloon—with the whisky.

Well, we got together outside, still breathing hard, and held a rump session by the front door. Whitey was there, of course, and me and two or three cow hands and the printer for the *Messenger,* who was celebrating on account of getting the paper out just one day late. We couldn't see inside; Whitey always kept the shades drawn and the place dim-lit.

"Boys," Whitey said, hearing a cork pop, "we got to get him out of there."

One of the cow hands—Pete his name was, Pete Gleeson—said, "I could open the door just a crack and shoot the skunk if I had sump'n to shoot him with."

"I can't have the place stunk up," Whitey said quick. "I gotta think about my customers. I gotta think about the hotel. Ain't anyone wants to drink or sleep in a stunk-up place." He gave us an anxious look.

"I couldn't guarantee to shoot him dead first crack," the cowpoke said.

"I figure the place is already stunk up," I told Whitey.

He put his nose to the keyhole. "Maybe not. I can't smell nothin' yet. Maybe that skunk's used to Shorty." He raised his voice. "If you don't come out, Shorty, I'll have to get the law." He waited for an answer. "I'll get the sheriff."

From inside we heard Shorty holler. "Way round 'em, Shep."

"That settles it. I will get the sheriff," Whitey said. "You fellers stand guard." He moved off down the street, making for the jail.

After a while he came back, bringing Sheriff McKenzie with him. I had an idea he had been chewing McKenzie's ear off on the way.

"All right, Sheriff," Whitey said when they came up to us.

McKenzie gnawed on his mustache. "Now, Whitey, let's augur on this. What you want me to do, anyway?"

"Get Shorty and the skunk outta my place of business, that's what," Whitey told him. "And no stink!"

"It's a big order, Whitey, a mighty big order," the sheriff said.

Whitey never did like the sheriff much. "The taxes I pay, looks like you would have an idea."

"Your paying taxes don't seem to help me much right now."

"You got a reputation as a fast man with a gun. Anyhow, you used to have. But watch you don't hit my new mirror."

McKenzie chewed his whiskers some more. "I don't know. I wouldn't say I was *that* fast."

Tubby Adams said, "Try persuadin'. Looks like Shorty would feel plumb agreeable by now."

The sheriff walked up to the door. "This here's the law, Shorty. This here's the sheriff. You gotta come outta there, Shorty. Best come peaceful. Best not make a stink."

What he got back was a song, or a piece of it. It sounded real pretty there in the dark.

> *"He's a killer and a hater!*
> *He's the great annihilator!*
> *He's a terror of the boundless prairie."*

"Don't look like I'm doin' any good," McKenzie said, turning around to us. He tried it again. "I don't want no trouble, Shorty. You gonna make me come in and git you?"

This time Shorty answered, "Yah."

The sheriff backed away. "This is serious, sure enough." He kept bitin' his whiskers and got an idea. "We'll just throw open the door and let the skunk come out by hisself."

We all looked at each other. It wasn't for nothin' we

had put McKenzie in the sheriff's office, you bet. Mc-
Kenzie put his hand on the knob while the rest of us got
ready to light out. Only the knob wouldn't turn. Shorty
wasn't as dumb as you might think.

"You get any smell?" Whitey asked.

McKenzie put his snout to the keyhole. "Yep."

"Oh, hell!"

"Rotgut," the sheriff said. "The stink of plain rotgut.
Nothin' else. Reckon that skunk's ashamed of his equip-
ment by comparison."

Tubby hitched his pants. "Long as you won't let anybody shoot that woods pussy, ain't nothin' to do but
starve Shorty out."

"Starve 'im out!" Whitey bawled. "Starve him out, you
damn fool! You think he'll want to eat?"

"I hadn't give proper thought to that," Tubby answered.

The printer swallowed another hiccup. "Have to wait
till the well runs dry."

Whitey clapped his hands to his head.

"I could use a drink myself," the sheriff put in.

Come to think of it, all of us could. From here on we
began to think deep.

I called the boys away from the door so's Shorty
couldn't hear. "Ain't there a way to poison skunks? What
they eat, anyhow?"

"Chickens," Tubby answered. "Damn 'em!"

"I hear tell they eat frogs and snakes," the printer said.

While we were thinking frogs and snakes, Shorty began
on another tune.

> *"Drink that rotgut, drink that rotgut,*
> *Drink that redeye, boys;*

It don't make a damn wherever we land,
We hit her up for joy."

"A frog now," Tubby said while he scratched his head with one hand. "Or snakes. Then there's the poison."

"I guess it ain't no trouble for you to put your hand on a frog or snake any old time," Whitey said.

"My boy's got himself a collection. I don't figger he'd mind partin' with a frog or a snake." Tubby licked his mouth. "Not in a good cause, anyway."

"It might work," the printer said. "Worth tryin'."

So Tubby said he'd get a frog, and Pete Gleeson—that was the cow hand—said he'd rout the druggist out and get some strychnine.

By and by they came back, Tubby holding a little old frog that was still mostly tadpole and Pete bringing powdered strychnine in a paper bag.

"First," said Sheriff McKenzie, taking charge of things, "we got to poison the frog. Pry his mouth open, one of you."

We gave the frog a good pinch of poison, with a drop of water for a chaser, and nosed him up to the crack and tried to goose him in. No go. That frog wouldn't budge.

After a while we found out it was because he was dead already.

"The frog idea ain't so good," the sheriff said. "Even with a live frog, it wouldn't work. A frog moves by hoppin'. How's he gonna hop *under* a door? Just bump his head, is all. Sump'n quick and slithery would be the ticket, like a snake."

"And don't poison him inside," I said. "Poison him out."

" 'Nother thing," Pete Gleeson put in. "Roll 'im in something sticky first, like flypaper."

You can see we was all thinkin' dry and hard.

Tubby went back to the house and got a garter snake, and Pete waked the druggist up again to get a sheet of flypaper. The druggist came along with him this time, figuring it wasn't any use to try to sleep.

Tubby and the sheriff didn't mind handlin' the snake.

The strychnine clung fine to the flypaper stickum, and the stickum clung fine to the snake. You never saw a snake like that one! All powdered up pretty, with a kind of a flounce around the neck where the strychnine was extra thick. You would have thought it was going to a wedding.

It could still crawl, though. Tubby pointed it at the crack and let go, and it slipped inside slick as butter.

Shorty was singing "Red Wing" now, only you could tell he had already sung his best and didn't have much class left in him.

"How long," asked Whitey, "does it take strychnine to work?"

The druggist chewed the question over with himself and came out with, "Depends."

"We'll give 'er plenty of time," Whitey said. "I won't open the place till mornin'."

"We done a lot of thinkin' for you," Tubby said, looking at Whitey sad-eyed. "Got a frog, too, and a snake."

"All right. All right, I'll set 'em up in the morning." Whitey talked as if it hurt him.

So we all dragged away, figuring, of course, to be on deck come opening time, which we were.

Whitey had the sheriff with him again, and there was

all the rest of us, plus quite a crowd who'd heard about the doings.

"Might have to break the door down," Whitey said. "I can't unlock her if she's locked from inside." He turned to McKenzie. "Sheriff, do your duty."

The sheriff waited a while, as if to show he wasn't taking orders from the likes of Whitey. Then he up and turns the knob and the door swung open.

It was just like we'd left it, the place was, except for a couple of empty bottles. No Shorty. No skunk. No snake. No nothing. It was just like we'd left it, except Whitey's new mirror was busted all to hell, which made us feel awful sorry for him. Business took up as usual.

* * *

Ray drained his glass. "I was tellin' the boys before you came in it was a stinkless skunk. Been separated from his ammunition, you might say, though we didn't know it, of course. The place didn't smell a bit worse than it does now."

"You mean the skunk ate the snake and went off and died, and so Shorty left?" I asked.

"Oh, no. That wasn't the way of it at all. What happened was we cured Shorty. He had picked up his skunk and lit out. Never touched a drop afterwards. He said he'd seen snakes plenty of times while drinkin', but by grab when he saw one with frostin' on it, it was time to quit."

MOUNTAIN
MEDICINE

~~~~~~

THE MIST along the creek shone in the morning sun, which was coming up lazy and half-hearted, as if of a mind to turn back and let the spring season wait. The cottonwoods and quaking aspens were still bare and the needles of the pines old and dark with winter, but beaver were prime and beaver were plenty. John Clell made a lift and took the drowned animal quietly from the trap and stretched it in the dugout with three others.

Bill Potter said, "If 'tweren't for the Injuns! Or if 'tweren't for you and your notions!" For all his bluster, he still spoke soft, as if on the chance that there were other ears to hear.

Clell didn't answer. He reset the trap and pulled from the mud the twig that slanted over it and unstoppered his goat-horn medicine bottle, dipped the twig in it and poked it back into the mud.

"Damn if I don't think sometimes you're scary," Potter went on, studying Clell out of eyes that were small and set close. "What kind of medicine is it makes you smell Injuns with nary one about?"

"Time you see as many of them as I have, you'll be scary too," Clell answered, slipping his paddle into the stream. He had a notion to get this greenhorn told off,

114

but he let it slide. What was the use? You couldn't put into a greenhorn's head what it was you felt. You couldn't give him the feel of distances and sky-high mountains and lonely winds and ideas spoken out of nowhere, ideas spoken into the head by medicines a man couldn't put a name to. Like now. Like here. Like this idea that there was brown skin about, and Blackfoot skin at that.

"I seen Blackfeet enough for both of us," he added. His mind ran back to Lewis and Clark and a time that seemed long ago because so much had come between; to days and nights and seasons of watching out, with just himself and the long silence for company; to last year and a hole that lay across the mountains to the south, where the Blackfeet and the Crows had fought, and he had sided with the Crows and got a wound in the leg that hurt sometimes yet. He could still see some of the Black-feet faces. He would know them, and they would know him, being long-remembering.

He knew Blackfeet all right, but he couldn't tell Bill Potter why he thought some of them were close by. There wasn't any sign he could point to; the creek sang along and the breeze played in the trees, and overhead a big eagle was gliding low, and nowhere was there a footprint or a movement or a whiff of smoke. It was just a feeling he had, and Potter wouldn't understand it, but would only look at him and maybe smile with one side of his mouth.

"Ain't anybody I knows of carries a two-shoot gun but you," Potter said, still talking as if Clell was scared over nothing.

Clell looked down at it, where he had it angled to his hand. It had two barrels, fixed on a swivel. When the top one was fired, you slipped a catch and turned the

other up. One barrel was rifled, the other bigger and
smooth-bored, and sometimes he loaded the big one with
shot, for birds, and sometimes with a heavy ball, for
bear or buffalo, or maybe with ball and buck both, just
for what-the-hell. There was shot in it this morning, for
he had thought maybe to take ducks or geese, and so re-
fresh his taste for buffalo meat. The rifle shone in the
morning sun. It was a nice piece, with a patch box a man
wouldn't know to open until someone showed him the
place to press his thumb. For no reason at all, Clell
called his rifle Mule Ear.

He said, "You're a fool, Potter, more ways than one.
Injuns'll raise your hair for sure, if it don't so happen I
do it myself. As for this here two-shooter, I like it, and
that's that."

Bill Potter always took low when a man dared him like
that. Now all he said was "It's heavy as all hell."

Slipping along the stream, with the banks rising steep
on both sides, Clell thought about beaver and Indians
and all the country he had seen—high country, pretty
as paint, wild as any animal and lonesome as time, and
rivers unseen but by him, and holes and creeks without a
name, and one place where water spouted hot and steam-
ing and sometimes stinking from the earth, and another
where a big spring flowed with pure tar; and no one believed him when he told of them, but called him the big-
gest liar yet. It was all right, though. He knew what he
knew, and kept it to himself now, being tired of queer
looks and smiles and words that made out he was half
crazy.

Sometimes, remembering things, he didn't see what
people did or hear what they said or think to speak when
spoken to. It was all right. It didn't matter what was said

about his sayings or his doings or his ways of thinking. A man long alone where no other white foot ever had stepped got different. He came to know what the Indians meant by medicine. He got to feeling like one with the mountains and the great sky and the lonesome winds and the animals and Indians, too, and it was a little as if he knew what they knew, a little as if there couldn't be a secret but was whispered to him, like the secret he kept hearing now.

"Let's cache," he said to Potter. The mist was gone from the river and the sun well up and decided on its course. It was time, and past time, to slide back to their hidden camp.

"Just got one more trap to lift," Potter argued.

"All right, then."

Overhead the eagle still soared close. Clell heard its long, high cry.

He heard something else, too, a muffled pounding of feet on the banks above. "Injuns!" he said, and bent the canoe into the cover of an overhanging bush. "I told you."

Potter listened. "Buffalo is all. Buffalo trampin' around."

Clell couldn't be sure, except for the feeling in him. Down in this little canyon a man couldn't see to the banks above. It could be buffalo, all right, but something kept warning, "Injuns! Injuns!"

Potter said, "Let's git on. Can't be cachin' from every little noise. Even sparrers make noise."

"Wait a spell."

"Scary." Potter said just the one word, and he said it under his breath, but it was enough. Clell dipped his paddle. One day he would whip Potter, but right now he reckoned he had to go on.

It wasn't fear that came on him a shake later, but just the quick knowing he had been right all along, just the holding still, the waiting, the watching what to do, for the banks had broken out with Indians—Indians with feathers in their hair, and bows and war clubs and spears in their hands; Indians yelling and motioning and scrambling down to the shores on both sides and fitting arrows to their bow strings.

Potter's face had gone white and tight like rawhide drying. He grabbed at his rifle.

Clell said, "Steady!" and got the pipe that hung from around his neck and held it up, meaning he meant peace.

These were the Blackfeet sure enough. These were the meanest Indians living. He would know them from the Rees and Crows and Pierced Noses and any other. He would know them by their round heads and bent noses and their red-and-green leather shields and the moccasins mismatched in color, and their bows and robes not fancy, and no man naked in the bunch.

The Indians waved them in. Clell let go his pipe and stroked with his paddle. Potter's voice was shrill. "You fool! You gonna let 'em torment us to death?"

That was the way with a mouthy greenhorn—full of himself at first, and then wild and shaken. "Steady!" Clell said again. "I aim to pull to shore. Don't point that there rifle 'less you want a skinful of arrows."

There wasn't a gun among the Indians, not a decent gun, but only a few rusty trade muskets. They had battle axes, and bows taken from their cases, ready for business, and some had spears, and all looked itching for a white man's hair. They waited, their eyes bright as buttons, their faces and bare forearms and right shoulders shining brown in the sun. Only men were at the shore line, but Clell could see the faces of squaws and young ones looking down from the bank above.

An Indian splashed out and got hold of the prow of the canoe and pulled it in. Clell stepped ashore, holding up his pipe. He had to watch Potter. Potter stumbled out, his little eyes wide and his face white, and fear showing even for an Indian to see. When he stepped on the bank, one of the Indians grabbed his rifle and wrenched it from him, and Potter just stood like a scared rabbit, looking as if he might jump back in the dugout any minute.

Clell reached out and took a quick hold on the rifle and jerked it away and handed it back to Potter. There was a way to treat Indians. Act like a squaw and they treated you bad; act like a brave man and you might have a chance.

Potter snatched the gun and spun around and leaped. The force of the jump carried the canoe out. He made a splash with the paddle. An arrow whispered in the air and made a little thump when it hit. Clell saw the end of it, shaking from high in Potter's back.

Potter cried out, "I'm hit! I'm hit, Clell!"

"Come back! Easy! Can't get away!"

Instead, Potter swung around with the rifle. There were two sounds, the crack of the powder and the gun-shot plunk of a ball. Clell caught a glimpse of an Indian going down, and then the air was full of the twang of bowstrings and the whispered flight of arrows, and Potter slumped slowly back in the canoe, his body stuck like a pincushion. An Indian splashed out to take the scalp. Two others carried the shot warrior up the bank. Already a squaw was beginning to keen.

Clell stood quiet as a stump, letting only his eyes move. It was so close now that his life was as good as gone. He could see it in the eyes around him, in the hungry faces, in the hands moving and the spears and the bows being raised. He stood straight, looking their eyes down, thinking the first arrow would come any time now, from anyplace, and then he heard the eagle scream. Its shadow lazed along the ground. His thumb slipped the barrel catch, his wrist twisted under side up. He shot without knowing he aimed. Two feathers puffed out of the bird. It went into a steep climb and faltered and turned head down and spun to the ground, making a thump when it hit.

The Indians' eyes switched back to him. Their mouths fell open, and slowly their hands came over the mouth holes in the sign of surprise. It was as he figured in that flash between life and death. They thought all guns fired a single ball. They thought he was big medicine as a marksman. One of them stepped out and laid his hand on Mule Ear, as if to draw some of its greatness into himself. A murmur started up, growing into an argument. They ordered Clell up the bank. When he got there, he saw one Indian high-tailing it for the eagle, and others following, so's to have plumes for their war bonnets, maybe, or to eat the raw flesh for the medicine it would give them.

There was a passel of Indians on the bank, three or four hundred, and more coming across from the other side. The man Clell took for the chief had mixed red earth with spit and dabbed it on his face. He carried a bird-wing fan in one hand and wore a half-sleeved hunting shirt made of bighorn skin and decorated with colored porcupine quills. His hair was a wild bush over his eyes and ears. At the back of it he had a tuft of owl feathers hanging. He yelled something and motioned with his hands, and the others began drifting back from the bank, except for a couple of dozen that Clell figured were head men. Mostly, they wore leggings and moccasins, and leather shirts or robes slung over the left shoulder. A few had scarlet trade blankets, which had come from God knew where. One didn't wear anything under his robe.

The squaws and the little squaws in their leather sacks of dresses, the naked boys with their potbellies and swollen navels, and the untried and middling warriors were all back now. The chief and the rest squatted down in a half circle, with Clell standing in front of them. They passed a pipe around. After a while they began to talk. He had some of the hang of Blackfoot, and he knew, even without their words, they were arguing what to do with him. One of them got up and came over and brought his face close to Clell's. His eyes picked at Clell's head and eyes and nose and mouth. Clell could smell grease on him and wood smoke and old sweat, but what came to his mind above all was that here was a man he had fought last season while siding with the Crows. He looked steadily into the black eyes and saw the knowing come into them, too, and watched the man turn back and take his place in the half circle and heard him telling what he knew.

They grunted like hogs, the Blackfeet did, like hogs about to be fed, while the one talked and pointed, arguing that here was a friend of their old enemies, the Crows. The man rubbed one palm over the other, saying in sign that Clell had to be rubbed out. Let them stand him up and use him for a target, the man said. The others said yes to that, not nodding their heads as white men would, but bowing forward and back from the waist.

Clell had just one trick left. He stepped over and showed his gun and pointed to the patch box and, waving one hand to catch their eyes, he sprang the cover with the other thumb. He closed the cover and handed the gun to the chief.

The chief's hands were red with the paint he had smeared on his face. Clell watched the long thumbnail, hooked like a bird claw, digging at the cover, watched the red fingers feeling for a latch or spring. While the others stretched their necks to see, the chief turned Mule Ear over, prying at it with his eyes. It wasn't any use. Unless he knew the hidden spot to press, he couldn't spring the lid. Clell took the piece back, opened the patch box again, closed it and sat down.

He couldn't make more medicine. He didn't have a glass to bring the sun down, and so to light a pipe, or even a trader's paper-backed mirror for the chief to see how pretty he was. All he had was the shot at the eagle and the patch box on Mule Ear, and he had used them both and had to take what came.

Maybe it was the eagle that did it, or the hidden cover, or maybe it was just the crazy way of Indians. The chief got up, and with his hands and with his tongue asked if the white hunter was a good runner.

Clell took his time answering, as a man did when making high palaver. He lighted his pipe. He said, "The white hunter is a bad runner. The other Long Knives think he runs fast. Their legs are round from sitting on a horse. They cannot run."

The chief grunted, letting the sign talk and the slow words sink into him. "The Long Knife will run." He pointed to the south, away from the creek. "He will run for the trading house that the whiteface keeps among the Crows. He will go as far as three arrows will shoot, and then he will run. My brothers will run. If my brothers run faster—" The chief brought his hand to his scalp lock.

The other Indians had gathered around, even the squaws and the young ones. They were grunting with excitement. The chief took Mule Ear. Other hands stripped off Clell's hunting shirt, the red-checked woolen shirt underneath, his leggings, his moccasins, his small-clothes, until he stood white and naked in the sun, and the squaws and young ones came up close to see what white flesh looked like. The squaws made little noises in their throats. They poked at his bare hide. One of them grabbed the red-checked shirt from the hands of a man and ran off with it. The chief made the sign for "Go!"

Clell walked straight, quartering into the sun. He walked slow and solemn, like going to church. If he hurried, they would start the chase right off. If he lazed along, making out they could be damned for all he cared, they might give him more of a start.

He was two hundred yards away when the first whoop sounded, the first single whoop, and then all the voices yelling and making one great whoop. From the corner of his eye he saw their legs driving, saw the uncovered brown skins, the feathered hair, the bows and spears, and then he was running himself, seeing ahead of him the far tumble and roll of high plains and hills, with buffalo dotting the distances and a herd of prairie goats sliding like summer mist, and everywhere, so that not always could his feet miss them, the angry knobs of cactus. South and east, many a long camp away where the Bighorn joined the Roche Jaune, lay Lisa's Fort, the trading house among the Crows.

He ran so as to save himself for running, striding long and loose through the new-sprouting buffalo grass, around the cactus, around the pieces of sandstone where snakes were likely to lie. He made himself breathe easy, breathe deep, breathe full in his belly. Far off in his feelings he felt the cactus sting him and the spines pull off to sting again. The sun looked him in the face. It lay long and warm on the world. At the sky line the heat sent up a little shimmer. There wasn't a noise anywhere except the thump of his feet and his heart working in his chest and his breath sucking in and out and, behind him, a cry now and then from the Indians, seeming not closer or farther away than at first. He couldn't slow himself with a look. He began to sweat.

A man could run a mile, or two or three, and then his breath wheezed in him. It grew into a hard snore in the throat. The air came in, weak and dry, and burned his pipes and went out in one spent rush while his lungs sucked for more. He felt as if he had been running on forever. He felt strange and out of the world, a man running in a dream, except that the ache in his throat was real and the fire of cactus in his feet. The earth spread away forever, and he was lost in it and friendless, and not a proper part of it any more; and it served him right. When a man didn't pay any mind to his medicine, but went ahead regardless, as he had done, his medicine played out on him.

Clell looked back. He had gained, fifty yards, seventy-five, half a musket shot; he had gained on all the Indians except one, and that one ran as swift and high-headed as a prairie goat. He was close and coming closer.

Clell had a quick notion to stop and fight. He had an idea he might dodge the spear the Indian carried and come to grips with him. But the rest would be on him before he finished. It took time to kill a man just with the hands alone. Now was the time for the running he had saved himself for. There was strength in his legs yet. He made them reach out, farther, faster, faster, farther. The pound of them came to be a sick jolting inside his skull. His whole chest fought for air through the hot, closed tunnel of his throat. His legs weren't a part of him; they were something to think about, but not to feel, something to watch and to wonder at. He saw them come out and go under him and come out again. He saw them weakening, the knees bending in a little as the weight came on them. He felt wetness on his face, and reached up and found his nose was streaming blood.

He looked over his shoulder again. The main body of Indians had fallen farther back, but the prairie goat had gained. Through a fog he saw the man's face, the chin set high and hard, the black eyes gleaming. He heard the moccasins slapping in the grass.

Of a sudden, Clell made up his mind. Keep on running and he'd get a spear in the back. Let it come from the front. Let it come through the chest. Let him face up to death like a natural man and to hell with it. His feet jolted him to a halt. He swung around and threw up his hands as if to stop a brute.

The Indian wasn't ready for that. He tried to pull up quick. He made to lift his spear. And then he stumbled and fell ahead. The spear handle broke as the point dug in the ground. Clell grabbed at the shaft, wrenched the point from the earth and drove it through the man. The

Indian bucked to his hands and knees and strained and sank back. It was as easy as that.

Bending over him, Clell let his chest drink, let his numb legs rest, until he heard the yells of the Indians and, looking up, saw them strung out in a long file, with the closest of them so close he could see the set of their faces. He turned and ran again, hearing a sudden, louder howling as the Indians came on the dead one, and then the howling dying again to single cries as they picked up the chase. They were too many for him, and too close. He didn't have a chance. He couldn't fort up and try to stand them off, not with his hands bare. There wasn't any place to hide. He should have listened to his medicine when it was talking to him back there on the creek.

Down the slope ahead of him a river ran—the Jefferson Fork of the Missouri, he thought, while he made his legs drive him through a screen of brush. A beaver swam in the river, its moving head making a quiet V in the still water above a dam. As he pounded closer, its flat tail slapped the water like a pistol shot, the point of the V sank from sight, and the ripples spread out and lost themselves. He could still see the beaver, though, swimming under water, its legs moving and the black tail plain, like something to follow. It was a big beaver, and it was making for a beaver lodge at Clell's right.

Clell dived, came up gasping from the chill of mountain water, and started stroking for the other shore. Beaver lodge! Beaver lodge! It was as if something spoke to him, as if someone nudged him, as if the black tail pulled him around. It was a fool thing, swimming under water and feeling for the tunnel that led up into the lodge. A fool thing. A man got so winded and weak that he didn't know medicine from craziness. A fool thing. A man couldn't force his shoulders through a beaver hole. The point of his shoulder pushed into mud. A snag ripped his side. He clawed ahead, his lungs bursting. And then his head was out of water, in the dark, and his lungs pumped air.

He heard movement in the lodge and a soft churring, but his eyes couldn't see anything. He pulled himself up, still hearing the churring, expecting the quick slice of teeth in his flesh. There was a scramble. Something slid along his leg and made a splash in the water of the tunnel, and slid again and made another splash.

His hands felt sticks and smooth, dry mud and the softness of shed hair. He sat up. The roof of the lodge just cleared his head if he sat slouched. It was a big lodge, farther across than the span of his arms. And it was as dark, almost, as the inside of a plugged barrel. His hand crossing before his eyes was just a shapeless movement.

He sat still and listened. The voices of the Indians sounded far off. He heard their feet in the stream, heard the moccasins walking softly around the lodge, heard the crunch of dried grass under their steps. It was like something dreamed, this hiding and being able to listen and to move. It was like being a breath of air, and no one able to put a hand on it.

After a while the footsteps trailed off and the voices faded. Now Clell's eyes were used to blackness, the lodge was a dark dapple. From the shades he would know it was day, but that was all. He felt for the cactus spines in his feet. He had been cold and wet at first, but the wetness dried and the lodge warmed a little to his body. Shivering, he lay down, feeling the dried mud under his skin, and the soft fur. When he closed his eyes he could see the sweep of distances and the high climb of mountains, and himself all alone in all the world, and, closer up, he could see the beaver swimming under water and its flat tail beckoning. He could hear voices, the silent voices speaking to a lonesome man out of nowhere and out of everywhere, and the beaver speaking, too, the smack of its tail speaking.

He woke up later, quick with alarm, digging at his dream and the noise that had got mixed with it. It was night outside. Not even the dark dapple showed inside the lodge, but only such a blackness as made a man feel himself to make sure he was real. Then he heard a snuffling of the air, and the sound of little waves lapping in the tunnel, and he knew that a beaver had nosed up and smelled him and drawn back into the water.

When he figured it was day, he sat up slowly, easing his muscles into action. He knew, without seeing, that his feet were puffed with the poison of the cactus. He crawled to the tunnel and filled his lungs and squirmed into it. He came up easy, just letting his eyes and nose rise above the water. The sun had cleared the eastern sky line. Not a breath of air stirred; the earth lay still, flowing into spring. He could see where the Indians had flattened the grass and trampled an edging of rushes, but there were no Indians about, not on one side or the other, not from shore line to sky line. He struck out for the far shore.

Seven days later a hunter at Fort Lisa spotted a figure far off. He watched it for a long spell, until a mist came over his eyes, and then he called to the men inside the stockade. A half dozen came through the big gate, their rifles in the crooks of their arms, and stood outside and studied the figure too.

"Man, all right. Somep'n ails him. Look how he goes."

"Injun, I say. A Crow, maybe, with a Blackfoot arrer in him."

"Git the glass."

One of them went inside and came back and put the glass to his eye. "Naked as a damn jay bird."

"Injun, ain't it?"

"Got a crop of whiskers. Never seed a Injun with whiskers yet."

"Skin's black."

"Ain't a Injun, though."

They waited.

"It ain't! Yes, I do believe it's John Clell! It's John Clell or I'm a Blackfoot!"

They brought him in and put his great, raw swellings of feet in hot water and gave him brandy and doled out roast liver, and bit by bit, that day and the next, he told them what had happened.

They knew why he wouldn't eat prairie turnips afterward, seeing as he lived on raw ones all that time, but what they didn't understand, because he didn't try to tell them, was why he never would hunt beaver again.

THE KEEPER
OF THE KEY

THE MAN wasn't bothering anybody. He just sat at one of those little tables in the bar at the Moon Dance House, trying to hold himself together, and by and by he gave up and laid his head on his crossed arms and went to sleep.

It wasn't long until the town marshal came in, looking full of business. He spotted the man and went over to him and prodded him awake and led him away.

"The new marshal's too darn far up in the collar," George Jackson said, watching them go out the door. "Things ain't like they were in the good old days."

George and Ray Gibler and I were at the big round table having a short one.

"You're headed the wrong way, son," Ray said to George. He lifted his glass and sighted through it. "The old days are coming back. I seen the time it was risky even to soup up a beer, especially if you had a little Indian blood in you."

"Sure. Prohibition," I said.

"Nup. It was a long way back."

"I know, and we were just pups and all that stuff. So now you can go ahead."

A grin cut creases in Ray's leathery face. "You sure

130

like to cut away the underbrush, so's a man can't sneak up on a story."

"Well," George said, when Ray didn't go on, "we're listening."

" 'Member old Judge McCoos?"

I answered, "Just barely."

Ray fired his pipe and hitched himself into a slouch in his chair and began to talk. . . .

Maybe you remember, Judge McCoos was a harness maker and a good one. He was the justice of the peace besides; and even if he didn't know any law, he had a couple of old law books on the desk in the back of his shop where he held court, though I never seen him break 'em open.

A Dutchman, I guess he was, with a nose like an Idaho spud and ears as big as roundup flapjacks. But for all that spread of ear he couldn't hear thunder, and so he carried an outsize horn for people to plead guilty into. I think it was those ears not hearing that first showed me size wasn't everything.

He set a lot of store by his court, the judge did. He took it serious, and everybody else better do the same, you bet. When he sat behind that old desk and pointed that horn out, you would think he was man and God both, and sometimes I believe he got a little mixed up himself. There wasn't many cases came before him, but sometimes maybe a half-breed would steal a little something or start a fight or get his nose so wet even the town marshal took notice of it.

So one day the judge said to me, "Ray, I have to be out of town for maybe a week, and there's some work in the shop that maybe people will be calling for, so I got to give the key to somebody."

I said, "How's justice going to get done while you're away, Judge?"

"How's that?" he came back, turning the horn on me. I yelled my question into it.

"Justice can wait," he answered back. "Hayin' can't." He put his hand up to one of those flapjack ears and gave it a pull. "You got time to watch the shop, Ray?"

I said I didn't, which wasn't so far from the truth.

He pulled the ear again. "You guess Frank Newcomb can stay sober that long?"

"It would be hard on him."

"How's that?"

"Sure," I said. "Sober as a judge."

"He's a good-enough man, sober," Judge McCoos said, "and we're friendly, and besides, who else has the time for it?"

Which was a question, all right. Old Frank Newcomb, now, he didn't have much but time—time and a fine appetite for the bottle. Frank had punched cows and skinned a freight team and worked at the livery stable off and on, but not for very long anywhere on account of it kept him from the bar. He used to call himself a humble drinkin' man, though I've seen humbler fellows.

"Seeing you can't keep the key yourself," the judge said, "could you kind of ride herd on Frank for me while I'm out of town?"

"I'll try," I told him, "but I can't guarantee results."

Judge McCoos waggled his head slow and said, "I guess I'll turn the key over to him." He took the horn out of his ear, rubbed that big nose of his, and went back to mending harness.

So the judge gave old Frank Newcomb the key and went off somewhere, and that's when things started to happen.

Frank was bright as a button that first day, handing out hame straps and bellybands and breechin' and passing the time of day with folks and building up good will for the shop. He was quite a feller. He had eyes as blue as a good trout hole, all tracked round with wrinkles that made him look real sociable; and what hair he hadn't shed was red and kind of bristly. He had a good stomach on him, too, that swelled against his lower vest, if he happened to have it buttoned, and spilled over his belt and never gave him any trouble no matter how he used it.

Along late that first day, though, a stranger came in and bought a saddle and laid the money down. It wasn't every day a man bought a saddle, nor put cash on the barrel head, either, and Frank set out pronto to celebrate the stroke of business he'd done for the judge. With the seventy-five dollars the saddle brought, he had the ammunition for quite a celebration, even allowing for the new and steeper prices Whitey Hanson was charging for what he called whisky.

I saw Frank that night and I saw him next day and I saw him off and on throughout, and his condition, while the money lasted, remained about the same, meaning he couldn't feel any better no matter what. I guess being in the judge's shoes gave him ideas, too, or maybe it was just that he knew he had quite a load aboard and better steer careful—anyhow, he talked solemner than usual and walked in a mighty dignified way.

It didn't take him long to spend the saddle money, especially after he began to expand and buy drinks for the house.

The comedown was pretty sad. There Frank was—the night of the third day after he sold the saddle—standing alone at the back end of the bar like moochers do, trying to get in a private word with Whitey. Whitey made out not to see him; and if he did happen to send his eye that way, he kept it cold and fishy. No one was offering to set 'em up, figuring they had taken their turn with Frank.

Frank edged along the bar so's to catch Whitey's ear, and then Whitey gave him the treatment he always gave moochers, trying to shame him out of the place. "No," he said in a loud voice while he shined a glass, "I won't give you no drink. You nicked me for three a'ready."

Frank kept his voice down. "I done spent a whole saddle here."

"And got value received."

Tubby Adams was up toward the head of the bar working on a beer, and he couldn't keep from putting his oar in. "I can't go along on that," he said. "No one gets value received, not at the prices you're chargin' now."

Whitey came back with, "Business is business." Whitey was what you would call a prudent man, if you wanted to be extra polite, and a good risk in banking circles. You could almost look at him and tell that. He had a broad forehead and his chin came to a point and the mouth above it was close and neat as a bullet hole. He had a pale face and hair.

"Business may be business," Tubby said, poking some of his stomach into his belt, "and whisky's supposed to be whisky, but I seen some I doubted."

Frank said, "Damn it, I'll pay you tomorrow."

"You got no idea what my expenses are," Whitey said,

talking to Tubby. "And taxes! You ought to see my tax bill!"

"Don't you get value received?" I asked.

Whitey let out a snort. "Nothin'. I get nothin'. Let someone get to feeling his oats and start a fight or something in here! You think I can find the sheriff or the marshal or anybody? I pay 'em for loafin', that's what."

"You gonna gimme that drink?" Frank asked.

Whitey turned to him. "I wouldn't be doin' you a favor, Frank," he said. "What you need is to lay off for a spell."

"Funny," Tubby said to Whitey. "You don't never think what's good for a man until his money runs out."

Frank had drawn himself up. "I ain't gonna beg, damn you, Whitey! And when I ask for a free one, all you got to say is no and leave off the sermon, hear? You're a nickel-nurser, that's what, and preachin' comes pore out of that twenty-two-caliber mouth of yours."

"That," I said, "is worth a drink," and I bought a round.

Next morning I called around at the shop and found Frank looking low in the mind, like as if he knew, barrin' a miracle, he would have to sober up. With him was Lem Bower, the marshal, who was a kind of a rabbit of a man who had got into office because it seemed so unlikely he'd ever shoot anyone. Lem looked a little bottle-worn himself.

Frank was at the judge's desk, thinking heavy. By and by he said, "Five and five makes ten."

Lem said, "There ain't no denyin' that."

"It depends," I answered back. "What does five pints of whisky and five bushels of oats make?"

"It makes life worth livin' and leaves something over

for the horse," Frank said. "But it's money I'm talkin' about."

When I kept quiet, he came back with, "About that five I borried from you. And about the five more I'd like to borry."

"Frank," I said, "I just can't spare it, that's all. And, seeing you haven't spent any saddle with me, maybe *I* can say you better taper off. The judge'll be back in a day or so."

"That's what I wanted the five for, to taper off on. You think I figure to stay drunk?"

"Maybe I could borry five from you, Ray," Lem put in.

Frank said, "He's good as gold."

I said again I couldn't spare it.

Frank took to thinking again. "That damn Whitey!" he said. "I spend a fancy saddle on him, and he treats me like a bum."

He put a hand out and it came to rest on one of the judge's law books, and he said, "You don't know no one wants to buy a saddle?"

I told him I didn't.

"We got some dandies."

I bobbed my head.

"We could put a sale on. Maybe we ought to put a sale on. Things just ain't movin'."

He put his chin in the hand that wasn't on the law book. "That Whitey! Cryin' about expenses and taxes and no service and all."

From outside we heard boots on the board sidewalk and voices laughing, and then the boots and the voices fading off in the direction of Whitey's.

"It's them half-breeds from the canyon," I said. "I saw 'em bringing in some loads of logs."

"Spendin' their logs on Whitey, like I spent the saddle," Frank said. "He gets people drunk and takes their money and then cuts their water off."

He kept on thinking, speaking slow as things came to him. "Some people got no business with liquor, like them Indians. Liquor's a white man's drink and Indians can't handle 'er like we can."

"Some of us don't do so good," I told him, but he wasn't listening to me.

"If that there money's got to be spent for liquor, it ought to be us spendin' it," he said. "Like as not, them breeds'll get a snootful and fall to fightin'."

He sat quiet for a long time, and I had a feeling he had almost put two and two together. "They'll fall to fightin'," he said, "and no one there to help Whitey, and him payin' high taxes."

His eyes slid over to the hand on the law book, and the chicken-track wrinkles closed around his eyes and then opened up, and there in his face I could see the idea. "Lem," he said to the marshal, "where's the judge keep the warrant book?"

Lem hitched the choke-bore pants he wore and spit at the stove and stepped over to the desk and dug around in a drawer and came out with a pad.

I knew, but still I asked, "What you aim to do, Frank?"

"I'm gonna help them breeds and give Whitey some service, too, so's he can't cry about gettin' nothing for his tax money."

"Supposin' you collect a fine," I said. "It wouldn't do you any good. The money wouldn't be yours. You got to account for it."

"Ray," he said, after thinking things over, "I won't fine

'em. I'll just collect costs—and costs go to me and the marshal."

"Right," Lem said, perking up.

"You ain't in authority," I went on. "You just got the key to the shop."

"Never you mind about that. I got the law on my side, ain't I, Lem? You're with me, ain't you, Lem? You and that there forty-four?"

Lem straightened out of his rabbit's hunch and slapped the old revolver that was rusted in the holster. "I go by papers," he said. "Gimme a paper, and I got to serve 'er."

Frank began to write. "I'll make 'em all out John Doe," he said to Lem, "and any breed who's drunk you bring 'im in." He scribbled some more. "And any looks like he's about to get drunk, you bring him in, too. This court will nip drinkin' in the bud, and give pore old Whitey some service, to boot." Before he finished, he was writing with a sure-enough flourish. "Law enforcement, that's what people pays their good tax money for."

He handed the warrants to Lem. "Officer," he said, real solemn, "do your duty."

"Yes, your honor," Lem said.

He made quite a roundup, Lem did. There were five John Does in his haul, and one of them might have been a little bit drunk. And some other people trailed in to see what went on, for I guess this was the first and last full-sized raid the town ever had. The back room of the harness shop wouldn't hold more'n a dozen or so people, and it was brimful, especially after Tubby Adams squeezed in, breathing hard from walking. Another who came in was Jordan Fredericks, who was a lawyer and high-educated but didn't take himself too important.

When they were all in, Frank Newcomb brought his stomach up from his belt and looked around with those blue eyes, serious as a barn owl, and knocked on the desk with his knuckles. "Oh yeah, oh yeah," he called out, "this honorable court is now in session, so help me God." He pointed to one of the prisoners. "You're drunk. Five dollars."

The Indians just stood there, not saying anything. Maybe this business didn't seem any crazier than some other white men's doings.

Jordan Fredericks said, sober-sided, "It doesn't seem that a case has been made out, your honor. No proof has been presented, no evidence heard. As a friend of the court, I'm sure it doesn't wish to be arbitrary."

Old Frank squirmed in his chair and ran a hand through his thin bristle of hair. I guess he hadn't figured on having a lawyer in the crowd. He said, "O.K. I mean, all right. But the court's got eyes and it's got ears, and it don't aim to see justice drag along." He waggled a finger at the breed. "Come here. You been drinkin', haven't you? You havem drink? Yes? No?"

The breed gave him a happy nod.

"Lemme smell your breath." Frank smelled of it.

"It is well known," Jordan Fredericks put in, "that alcohol has no odor to one who has himself partaken— even moderately, your honor."

"You smell him," Frank said to Lem, but Lem just looked unhappy and shook his head.

"Who ain't had a drink?" Frank called out. "Anyone here ain't had a drink?"

It was a long minute before anyone spoke up, and then Tubby Adams said, kind of apologetic, "My stomach's been cuttin' up lately."

"Come and take a whiff," Frank ordered. "Whisky, ain't it?"

"Anyhow, it's what Whitey Hanson passes off for whisky at a fancy price," Tubby said.

"Five dollars," said Frank. "And I hope the local bar is satisfied that proper evidence has been took. Five dollars, you! You gottem five bucks?"

The man did. He looked around first, like he didn't know what was going on, and then he fumbled a bill out of his pants and handed it to Frank.

"Next case," said Frank. He pointed to another man and said, "You're drunk."

It sure was an expeditious court. In less'n fifteen minutes Frank had twenty-five dollars.

Just as he collected the last five, there was a commotion in the front of the shop and a squeezing at the door to the back part, and in came Whitey Hanson. "Damn you, Frank!" he said, looking around kind of wild. "What's the big idea?"

"Law enforcement," Frank said. "Service."

"The devil!" Whitey broke out. "You come in and arrest my customers and take their money, and it's hard on business, and I got taxes to pay."

"Whitey," Frank said, fixing that blue eye on him, "that's what we're doin'—givin' you service for your tax money. Damned if this honorable court ain't surprised at you!"

Whitey said, "You're drunk yourself."

"Not on what *you* treated me to."

"You're drunk and a nuisance," Whitey yelled.

I guess Frank knew we were all with him, for he sure acted bold. He beat on the desk. "Order!" he yelled back. "Marshal, see we have order!"

Lem moved toward Whitey while he patted his holster.

There was a little time of quiet then, while Frank looked at Whitey. "Mr. Hanson," he said, "the court heard you say nuisance, and there is such a thing as a nuisance—I mean accordin' to law." His face turned to Jordan Fredericks. "Ain't I right, Jordan?"

Jordan said, "Right, your honor."

"You been maintainin' a nuisance, Mr. Hanson, in that drinking place of yours," Frank went on. "It takes sheriffs and marshals to keep order, and a lot of people are complainin' about how you run your place. Yes, sir, it's a plumb nuisance and no evidence needed, the court speaking out of what it knows by itself." He looked at Jordan again.

Jordan rubbed his mouth straight. "The court may act in its wisdom," he said, "but if witnesses are needed, I'm sure there are plenty here to testify for the prosecution." He looked around and we all began to nod, even the breeds joining in when they saw what the style was.

"What the hell!" Whitey shouted.

Frank rapped again. "Order! This here court's got to fine you, Mr. Hanson."

Whitey shouted again. His pale face had come to look like liver.

"And another thing," Frank said, for he was in full swing now. "You charge too much for that rotgut, way too much. You ask too much from pore fellers like these, who got no business drinkin', anyway. Liquor, the way you sell it, ain't within the reach of a lot of people. What you're doin' is—is—" He looked at Jordan Fredericks. "Gimme a name for it."

"Extortion," said Fredericks.

Frank picked up the word. "Extortion—plain and

fancy extortion. Nuisance and extortion both." He patted the law book. "You got to pay twenty-five dollars." His eye happened on me, and he added, "Costs, all costs."

Whitey cried out, "You're crazy! This is a kangaroo court."

"This honorable court don't like to be insulted," Frank said.

Jordan Fredericks gave him the cue. "Contempt."

"Yes, sir, contempt," Frank said. "Contempt o' court. And that makes five dollars more, and if you don't act and charge more reasonable, the court'll have you up again."

I figured we would need a doctor for Whitey. His face was red as a new barn, and he kept gulping. He looked around, and what he seen didn't give him comfort, for there wasn't anyone thought too high of him, and we were sure-God all with the court, kangaroo or whatever.

Whitey wasn't dumb, regardless. He saw the way things were and figured he better take it graceful; and, being the kind of feller he was, he thought about what would be good business in the long run. So at last he did his best to smile, and he put a ten and a twenty on the desk and said, "I guess I know when I'm licked. Come on. The house'll set 'em up."

Almost before he finished, Frank said, "Court's let out."

It was a real successful session.

Judge McCoos was fit to be tied when he got back and heard about things, but he had to wait a week before he could be sure his sentiments would sink into Frank. Then he really told him off. Travesty on justice was one of the things he said, and corruption of an honorable court and all. And, for another thing, what about that seventy-five-dollar saddle?

It busted up their friendship.

And then again it was the making of Frank Newcomb.

Ray lifted his drink and took the last sip and sat fiddling with the glass afterwards.

"How did it make Frank Newcomb?" George asked.

"Well, you see, next election Frank run against Judge McCoos, and damn if he didn't beat him hands down."

"I can believe everything but that," I said.

"It was just the simple workings of politics," Ray explained. "Frank got the reform vote, or that part of it that didn't savvy things, and then he got the vote that didn't like Whitey Hanson."

"And that elected him?"

"Nope. Not alone. It was really the breed vote. McCoos always charged them ten dollars, instead of five, for getting drunk, and, naturally, they went to the bargain counter."

THE FOURTH
AT GETUP

~~~~~~

It was the Fourth of July there in Getup, Montana, and we had just had a parade that everyone said was pretty good even if a little long on ranch machinery and saddle stock and short on fancy works.

The rodeo would come later. Now people were just milling around, shouting hello and having some horseplay the way they do when they are feeling free and easy. Everyone in the county was there—ranchers and ranch hands, dude wranglers, bronc stompers, townspeople, men, women and children. They crowded the sidewalks and spilled out into the street and laughed and yelled and dodged the firecrackers that the small fry were popping in spite of the marshal. Overhead, pennants and bunting were flapping patriotically to a breeze that kept sifting the dust around.

I had put my horse down in the stockyards corral after the parade and was pushing up the street, stopping every once in a while to shake hands with locals I hadn't seen in nine or ten months, my winter quarters then being in Kentucky, when a lady I recognized as a tourist even without the slacks appeared out of the crowd and called my name, putting Mister ahead of it. While she took in my outfit of cowboy boots, red shirt and broad-brimmed hat, it came to me that she was a passing acquaintance from the Bluegrass State. She had three lady friends in tow, whom she identified as fellow residents. I would have known they weren't Montanans anyway. Here wind and weather put their brand on face and hair, and girls too big for slacks, if they wear them at all, manage to wear them without the appearance of defiance in front and apology behind.

"We were just passing through on the way to Glacier Park," my acquaintance said, "and we ran into the parade and, of all things, spied you riding in it. We're going to stay for the rodeo. We've never seen one."

"I've never been west before," another of the ladies said. "Is it—" she made a helpless little sweeping gesture with one hand while she tried for the right words—"is it all like this?"

To the east the bare hills, tan as panther hide, climbed from the valley and leveled into benchlands that ran treeless out of sight. South, a couple of bald buttes nosed for the sky. To the west, twenty miles beyond a vacant lot grown up with gumweed, the main range of the Rockies reared, blue and purple with distance, stone and persevering pine. One of the cottonwoods that flanked Main Street had decked the lady's hair with a wisp of down.

"All the same," I answered—but I knew she was thinking of cozy confines, of soft verdure, of bluegrass lately bloomed, of oak and maple and sweet gum and maybe of a colt by Bull Lea frisking in a paneled pasture.

"Look," I went on to them all, "my wife will want to see you. She's around somewhere." I didn't tell them she would be either at the drugstore or the bar, the odds being in favor of the bar. There were just those places to look. Everything else was buttoned up.

I bunched the four ladies and got them going and, just on the chance, stuck my head in the drugstore, but, barring a thousand kids, there wasn't anyone inside except people who were celebrating by pulling on chocolate malts.

I hazed my four ladies up the street toward the bar. I wished it was designated by "Lounge" or "Cocktails," but it wasn't. In Montana we went as far as we could go when we changed saloons into bars.

It was noisy outside, from noises inside and out, and the ladies looked at one another and then at me, asking was it really all right.

I pushed them on in.

The place was thick—men and a few women crowded along the bar itself, men and women at the tables on the other side, men and women standing in the middle, all jawing and laughing and sometimes clapping one another on the back. One of the women had a baby in her arms. When we passed her, she was trying to get the baby to call the bartender Jelly Belly.

The lady who had asked if the West was all alike turned back with some flutter and said to me, "I never!"

I told her it was all right, but even as I squinted around for my wife I was back in Kentucky with the lady, sitting on a columned porch, and colored boys with white jackets and soft voices were serving mint juleps made by Irvin Cobb's recipe, and the talk was of ancestors and landholders and James Lane Allen, of old and established and perished yet imperishable things, of the antecedents that made a region and, making it, made it comfortable. Not caste-bound but correct and comfortable, you all know.

While I was scanning the faces, a friend who was only part Indian but might have had his face on a nickel came up and threw his arm across my shoulders and told me, as he had many a time before, that his dad was one of the best friends Charlie Russell, the painter, ever had, and I could ask Charlie if it wasn't so except Charlie was dead. And don't think he was drunk, either, or anyhow not drunk enough to be telling lies.

I had to reassure the ladies again.

My wife was in the back room, which was closed off from the front by an open doorway eight feet wide. With her were six or eight others, including her mother and her father, who was known to everyone as Tom and who was the last of the rugged individualists except for Hoover. They were seated at the round table used for pinochle on duller days. The ladies were sipping on beers and the men were drinking highballs or shots. The men all had their hats on. In rural Montana you don't uncover except in the presence of the flag or the dead and not always then.

My wife recognized the acquaintance from Kentucky and greeted her and got introduced to the other ladies and started presenting them to the gang at the table.

One of the crowd was a man named Tippy who had had quite a few considering the time was not yet noon. When it came his turn to meet the ladies, he pushed back his chair and got up, saying by George he had never kissed a girl from Kentucky. He managed to grab the nearest lady's hand. He pulled her to him and smacked her on the cheek. Her partners edged back out of range.

We pulled up more chairs, and Tom motioned to the

bartender, who came up and said, "What'll it be, ladies and gents?" In Getup most people, men at any rate, drink ditches, which is short for ditchwaters, which is short for ditchwater highballs, which means bar whisky and tap water.

While they were ordering a man came in and stood quiet. He began to glower while I tried to remember him. I got up and went over and shook hands.

"I'm sorry," I said. "I remember you, but not your name."

"The holy hell you don't! You used to!"

I could see that the visiting ladies heard him.

"It'll come to me," I said. "What you been doin'?"

"Same as usual." He considered "same as usual" for a while. "I've done more'n my share of hard work. I'm through with it. Writin' must be nice." He stood there with some hard resentment in him, with all the noise and whirl around him, and looked at the hard work he had done, stacking hay, feeding cattle, building fence, helping with the lambing and the calving. He couldn't have done much of anything else, not from his looks.

A lame-armed old man in old coveralls got me out of that hole. He broke in on us, telling me one arm was still gimpy all right, but the other was good. He gave my wrist a hard twist.

The bartender brought the drinks, and I saw that each of our visitors had her little piece of money on the table in front of her. I guess they had been traveling dutch. At about that time Tom saw the money, too, and said, "Naw! Naw!" to this outlandishness. Guests buying drinks, and women guests to boot! He thrust a bill on the bartender, and the ladies, murmuring protests, put their change back in their pocketbooks.

Soft stuff, they had ordered. The bottles at the sides of their glasses showed as much. Soft stuff! Soft stuff on the Fourth of July! So maybe they didn't sit on shaded porches and sip mint juleps and exclaim at Bull Lea's son. Maybe they belonged to the opposition, to the fundamentalist church and the missionary society and to the book club I'd heard about whose members in a moment of doubtful grace tried to identify the bad word in *Strange Fruit,* tried to identify it, since they were good ladies all, by means of secret, write-in nominations of which none hit the mark.

Of such was Kentucky, too. Or of such was the Bluegrass, along with whisky and horses and history. And they made one. Divided we stand, the saved and the damned united and all saved by dedication to custom and origin. Right now my wife and two of the ladies were talking, talking the polite, endless small talk, the on-and-on personality-talk that was part of the custom, the voices of the visitors sounding singularly soft and light and lovely after the flat harshnesses of the West.

Out in front a man yelled above the rest, calling someone a goddam son of a bitch. Except for the ladies, who tried not to, we didn't pay any attention. From the tone you could tell it was nothing to get excited about.

Now Tom saw what the visitors had ordered. To his protest they answered that they wanted to be themselves so that they could really enjoy the rodeo.

Tom lit a cigar and waved it at them. "Whisky don't hurt you here," he told them. "Country's so high and dry you burn it up quickly. You breathe it right out. Not like in them southern states where I shipped a carload of broncs once. You take three or four drinks in that climate, and they pile up on you, and first thing you know you're loco." He added, as if admitting a personal infirmity, "Beer's different anywhere. Beer bloats me."

This last might have been lost on them, for Del Crockett had ambled up. Del was a good guy who looked like something dredged up from the sea. He had, and still has, great, shiny eyes and a broad face and two outsize stomachs divided by his belt and a hand that looked as if it had just come out of the guts of a tractor. On his head was a hat that had peered up at many a crankcase and blown around a lot of corrals.

Right after he had been introduced, Del excused himself and sidled around the man who still stood glowering now and then at me. His object was the gents' room. Before he went in he took off his hat and hung it on a hook outside, as if this was a ceremony to uncover for.

Tippy was two drinks drunker. He saw Del's hat on the hook and got up, fairly steady, and ran over and plucked it off.

The man I didn't remember didn't move.

Tippy pranced back with the hat and insisted that one of the ladies take it. "It'll be a keepsake. Somep'n to recollect Getup by."

She took the edge of the brim between the tips of her thumb and forefinger and held the hat away from her. With a new sweatband it would have looked better inside.

The bartender came over.

"A little drink'll make you feel better," Tom said to the guests.

"Thank you, suh," one of them answered quickly, "but we feel mighty fine."

Del came out of the toilet and looked for his hat and didn't see it until he focused his gargoyle eyes on us. A big smile split his face then, and he came and took his hat from the lady and put it on his head.

"She wanted it for a keepsake," Tippy said. "Let her have it for a keepsake."

"Y'ever see the like of this?" Del asked the lady.

She shook her head.

"Just one big family," he said, and started patting her on the back with that big, thick, friendly crankcase hand.

A colored man walked through the open doorway from the front, bound for the gents' room. His name was Cowboy Lee, and not without reason. He could stick a bad horse with a loose-jointed grace that made the feat look simple. I spoke to him, and he answered easily, calling me by my first name.

Again my eye fell on the man who stood in moody silence, and all at once it came to me. I went to him. "Willie!" I said. "Willie Geggler! How long since we worked together on the old 5T?"

Willie's face softened, and a flicker of a smile came on it. "Been a long time, all right," he answered, and nodded and trailed into the other room.

Questions were swimming in the eyes of two of the ladies when I sat down. "Old friend," I said. "Willie Geggler." I didn't add that he had always been a little loco; all of us in Montana had the seeds of his insistence in us.

My two questioners looked around and then back at me, still questioning. I made a gesture to take in the place and all the people and all they had observed, and it was in me to explain with some high phrase like frontier democracy and to enlarge on it. "We're young here," I said and let it go at that and was at once glad and regretful that we were.

"You'll need to take it easy for a while after riding all them rodeo broncs," Tom told the visitors. It took them an instant to understand how he meant it. "Why don't you come by the house afterwards and see how home folks live?"

My mother-in-law seconded him.

"Thank you all so much," one of the ladies answered for the rest, "but I don't guess we'll have the time."

The ladies got up and, one by one, the men. The ladies said they had had a wonderful, a sure-enough wonderful time. Everyone shook hands with them. Tippy said he never had kissed a Kentucky girl good-by, either, not anyhow until then.

I took the visitors to the door. They were easier to get out than in.

Back in the back room the old man had to show me again how good his good arm was. My mother-in-law said it was time to think about lunch. Tippy told my wife the visitors were nice. Tom took the cigar from his mouth and looked at it and shook his head and said, "Sure takes all kinds of people all right." Then he ordered another round, whisky not hurting you in that high, dry climate.